Detective Daintypaws:
A Squirrel in Bohemia

ANDREW K. LAWSTON

DEDICATION

To my darling proncess, Melanie...
And of course, for Buscemi the KMS.
Your Scruffy and Blonde Staff love you so much.
Keep solving crimes, you lovely little kitten.

CONTENTS

ACKNOWLEDGMENTS

First, thanks and all my love to Melanie. Much of what you're about to read was inspired by our daily silliness over the last six years.

Thanks also to the crack team of early readers who convinced me that Buscemi's adventures could carry beyond the mean streets of Barnes.

Large chunks of this book were written in The Bridge over the last four years. Huge thanks to the whole team for indulging the quiet oddball in the corner.

Thanks to my parents – I think I actually finally have written something nice!

And of course, huge thanks to the real Buscemi Daintypaws Twinklefur, our Kitten Mitten Spitten.

1 DAY ONE

Bohemia was a pretentious place, even by the standards of South West London in the early 21st Century. It couldn't quite seem to make up its mind whether it was a wine bar or a delicatessen, and was renowned locally for being the place where you could get two glasses of tolerable red wine and a cheeseboard for £30. Opinions were divided on whether that was a good or a bad deal, and the division was drawn largely between those paying the money, and those taking it. But it was renowned nonetheless.

The establishment was perfectly suited for a central London hot spot. It would have been perfect if it had been tucked away down a side street in Soho; "creatives" with wafer-thin laptops would have flocked to its fashionably unfinished decor and splinter-studded tables. Which made it all the more unfortunate that it was *actually* situated in North Barnes, sandwiched between a hairdresser and the start of a row of mind-meltingly expensive but strangely drab terraced houses on Castelnau, the apparently endless avenue that ran from Hammersmith Bridge all the way down to the *Red Lion* pub.

It's perhaps fair to say, then, that *Bohemia* was a bit of

an anomaly. But they'd been open for over three years, which according to Barnes protocol was more than long enough to make them 'part of the community'. Certainly the appearance outside of three police cars that fateful Tuesday morning in early November was cause for concerned frowns to crease the foreheads of the community's largely self-appointed pillars. Though the frowns made little impact as most of those foreheads were already pre-creased from many long years of frowning at children playing on grassed areas, dogs barking at the 209 bus, and the establishment of a pizza parlour (of all things!) next to the newsagent.

The police were a frequent sight in Barnes, but were most often passing through from Hammersmith on the way to Roehampton. Their presence next to *Bohemia* demanded close scrutiny. Dogs were walked past the darkened shop at a snail's pace, to the obvious whimpering chagrin of the relevant canines. Shoppers who hadn't brought groceries from anyone but M&S and Ocado since Gordon Brown was Prime Minister suddenly felt a pressing need for a pint of milk from the convenience store three doors down. One particularly enterprising concerned citizen even braved the rickety jogger-choked footpaths over Hammersmith Bridge in order to buy eight copies of the *Big Issue*. He then put on his oldest coat and stood on the pavement opposite *Bohemia,* pretending to sell the magazine so he could try and get a good look.

He sold all eight copies in less than quarter of an hour, and then had to go home with his pockets jingling with loose change. It was a more than slightly humbling experience for a retired banker, but it was more coinage than he'd carried in several decades. A wild thought crossed his mind that he ought to bag up his earnings, find the nearest pub with a pool table, and take the young upstarts to billiards school. But he was fairly sure the nearest pool table was somewhere in Hounslow, the mere thought of which put paid to that plan.

These were all amateurs in the rubbernecking game, however. Before the first dog walker had picked up their lead and poo bags, and pulled on their sensible green wellies, Detective Buscemi was already on the scene.

Slipping gracefully under the police cordon tape, Buscemi greeted the uniformed constable stationed in front of *Bohemia*'s door. "What a morning! Let's hope the forensics boys finished with the coffee machine at least, am I right?"

The constable shuffled on his feet awkwardly.

"Come on constable, crack a smile. It won't kill anyone." Buscemi tossed her head. "Let's face it, judging by the amount of uniforms around here, that particular horse has long bolted."

The constable continued to avoid eye contact, rocking on his feet slightly.

Buscemi had run out of camaraderie, however. "Now look here, I'm sure you've been here since the crack of stupid o'clock, up with the sparrow's fart and all that, but this recalcitrant attitude *simply will not do*, do you hear me?"

The constable finally looked down and locked eyes with Buscemi for a tense moment. He cracked. He gave one last shifty glance to left and right before abandoning his post.

"Who's a pretty little kitten then?" he asked as he hunkered down to the pavement awkwardly, and scratched the small black cat between her ears, marvelling at her piercingly intelligent green eyes, and even at the flash of pure white fur on her throat that made her look like a particularly lovable vicar.

"Constable, this is completely unprofessional!" Buscemi protested, as she purred under the man's close-bitten fingernails. She judged from his technique that he was almost certainly staff for just one cat.

"Aren't you adorable?" the constable mumbled as he stroked Buscemi's ears, remembering to dart suspicious glances at each and every car that swished past.

"Yes, yes, of course I am," Buscemi snapped, "now let me in before the evidence gets contaminated by your clod-hopping pavement-shy confreres in the bin bag gear."

She scratched at *Bohemia's* door to underline her point. The constable risked severe flesh wounds by tutting. "Gosh, you can't come in here, moppety poppet. It's a crime scene."

Buscemi rolled her vivid green eyes. "Yes, that's why I'm here. It certainly wasn't just to get my ears mauled by a sausage-fingered tit. Now open the door before I say something regrettable about your mother's life choices. *Moppety poppet*, I ask you."

As Buscemi continued to dab her paw against the door, the constable's brow furrowed. "Oh dear, unless this is your home, of course. In which case your fur will be all over it already."

She barely remembered to suppress her shrug, as that always freaked out her staff. "OK, why not? Yes. I want my... kibble. Which is a damn stupid word, for the record. I live here, and I want my kibble."

The constable gave a sigh as he stood and pushed open the door. As Buscemi passed him he muttered "no need to be rude", which she thought was unreasonable as she'd made every effort to rub against the plod's trouser leg in her nearest approximation of gratitude.

Inside, *Bohemia* was crowded with police. They blocked her view of the framed prints by local artists that covered every inch of wall that didn't have a chalk-inscribed slate or a wine rack over it. Their urgent chatter drowned the commendably earnest bourgeoisie-comforting indie music droning from the radio. Their coats were all piled mercifully over the panini counter. Whatever serious crime had been committed, it had at least transformed this cafe from its usual vibe as a pushchair-infested den of wankers.

As she watched the forensics team moving around with the weird slow-motion grace of people who were basically dressed in bin liners, Buscemi couldn't quite shake her first thought that there had almost certainly never been so many people with real jobs inside *Bohemia* until that morning. It was unworthy of her, as thoughts went, but then they were covering so many pretentious fixtures with their bumbling.

The epicentre of their activity was a large area of painstakingly-distressed artisan floorboards, covered with a wide white plastic sheet, which was spattered with red like a raspberry ripple bath bomb. The sight of it made the velvet pads of Buscemi's paws tingle.

The door clicked shut behind her with the faintest click, and a shimmering jingle of cowbells. It might as well have been a gunshot, judging by the way the entire forensics team went from slow-motion to giving themselves whiplash inside their bin liner suits as they pirouetted to face the door.

She curled her tail around her hind legs as she sat on her haunches, and stared at them all. The bulky shape lying on the plastic sheet was almost forgotten.

As the silence dragged beyond bearable, Buscemi stretched. She flexed her claws. "Well. Whose trousers do I have to nuzzle to get some pancetta round here?"

"Who let this bloody cat in?" A copper was pointing right at Buscemi, tired eyes narrowing in sudden hostility. "What uniformed pillock let a bloody moggy wander into my crime scene?"

Buscemi watched the officer carefully, choking down her library of retorts. Cats understand matters of territorial etiquette better than anyone, and right now she realised she was firmly on this guy's patch. Even if he was using a racial slur.

"Pussy!" The faintly overdone Italian accent floated from behind the pile of coats covering the panini counter. "Mrs Pussy, you're back from your travels! Come to Antonio!"

Every hackle Buscemi possessed was raised and pointed at the voice's source, and she was at the point of actually hissing when a portly shape unfolded itself from the till into a vaguely human shape, and two deep brown eyes gazed at her, shot through with desperate pleading.

This guy is desperate and will totally give me bacon, Buscemi thought, pledging every shred of what passed in her book for allegiance to the flustered and scared proprietor of *Bohemia* as he walked round the counter to the door with his arms spread wide, though he wasn't quite daft enough to pick her up, or commit any other offences punishable by summary clawing.

Buscemi flicked her tail, and scurried between the man's legs, Cornetto, or whatever he said his name was. He sagged with relief and retreated back to the space behind the panini counter, forced to walk like John Wayne as the adorable little black cat orbited his ankles.

The copper threw up his hands in disgust and turned back to glower at the dust on the floor around the sheet.

Behind the counter, Buscemi stiffened as she felt Cornetto's finger touch her ears. "It is you, isn't it? The *clever* cat?"

Buscemi treated him to a contemptuous full body shudder. Compliments were a fine thing, but she was just two yards away from a real life murder scene, literally the most exciting thing she'd ever seen apart from the time there was that new bin behind the florist and she'd had to spend an hour just staring at it, and this guy was holding her up with nauseating fanboy behaviour. "Yes, probably. I prefer 'clever *crime-solving* cat'. And that's kind of a crime right there, so if you don't mind..."

She turned away but to her indignation, the man's forefinger hooked in her collar. He sank to his knees, stifling a yelp as he barked his shin on the chiller cabinet's power cable.

Cornetto looked at her with a plaintive frown. "I can't believe I'm hiring a cat detective, but I need this to go away."

Buscemi scoffed. "You've got a dead guy congealing on

your wanky floorboards. You'll need more than my help to make *that* go away. I already had breakfast this morning, I couldn't possibly. Unless he was made of smoked salmon and catnip, obviously."

"I know what you're thinking," Cornetto said abruptly, and Buscemi bristled at his presumption. "You're thinking a dead guy in my cafe is already a pretty big problem when police are swarming all over the place. But this is just... I don't know, just some guy who got into a fight and crawled in here to die or something. Drugs and so on, I expect. It's nothing to do with me, I'll be open again tomorrow and I'll be busier than ever answering customers' questions about how many of his internal organs we were able to see."

"Sweet, how many *can* you see?" Buscemi tried to turn again, but the man's finger was still hooked tight inside her collar.

"Forget this man!" the cafe owner pleaded. "He is nothing, a distraction."

"A distraction?" Buscemi narrowed her eyes with new interest. "Distracting from what?"

The man pulled an inspection panel from the back of his chiller. "In here, this is the sort of thing that can get a place closed down. Not some gang thug who happens to bleed out on your stripped pine floorboards."

Buscemi was tempted to take the uncaring brute to task over his callous disregard for life, but then a familiar smell hit every single receptor in her exquisitely-calibrated nose.

"Woah, you've got a dead squirrel in your chiller? That's awesome, I thought it was all brie and grape and quinoa in here! Hang on, isn't this Flollops? I knew this nutter!"

Cornetto dropped the panel which crashed into the floor with a heavy clang. He plastered an innocent smile over his face when the assembled police looked round. "A dead man is bad luck," he hissed, "but a dead squirrel looks like bad hygiene. They'd close me down. Can you do anything?"

Buscemi licked her lips. "Say no more. I've been looking for a case to get my teeth into."

Cornetto pulled her head away again. It was only the heavy CID presence that was saving him from a serious scratching, at this point.

"Find out what killed it, how it got here. Then I can plug up the hole, wherever it is, burn the body, and not have to worry about those environmental health bastards springing a surprise inspection on me any time soon."

Buscemi finally wriggled from Cornetto's grasp, and sat back on her haunches while the cafe owner replaced the heavy panel with some difficulty. "My first homicide case! And it's a locked fridge mystery! Brutal!"

Cornetto smiled as he watched the little black cat beginning to purr. "You're a real detective, aren't you? I'm sorry the police won't let you solve their case over there."

Buscemi was feeling unusually generous. "Oh that's fine, Mr Latteplease, it looks pretty routine to me. In fact, being as the two deaths happened in the same room, I'll probably solve that dead guy by accident or something. You know, in the *Course of my Enquiries*."

All she could think was, *I get to make enquiries! Sweet! This is even better than that time I attacked the Christmas tree!*

Without really knowing why, beyond being very stressed and a bit thirsty, Cornetto reached to the drinks chiller and popped the top from a bottle of Heineken. After a hefty settling swig, he reached forward and tucked the bottle's cap, complete with its red star logo, into Buscemi's collar.

"There! You've got a badge now. Like a proper sheriff. Ah, *detective*."

Detective Buscemi's chest swelled with pride. As an origin story, she decided, it wasn't half bad.

***

Bohemia's door swung shut behind her, to the increasing bemusement of the copper guarding it, and Buscemi wandered across the road in a bit of a daze, to the point where she barely noticed the 72 bus which missed her by barely the breadth of one of her twitchy whiskers. She had a badge! And a case! The little black cat who had dreamed for so long of becoming a real detective was now officially enlisted in the war on crime! She'd have to get herself some abrasive but ultimately endearing personality quirks, and everything!

"Screw the DA, and screw you, I get results," she tried to growl, but it came out as a heartbreakingly plaintive croaky miaow. She swished her tail dismissively. She could work on a drink problem or a love of classic cars instead.

Buscemi hopped up on the pavement in front of *Bohemia*'s rival deli that sat directly opposite, *Spoonful*. Why couldn't *they* have had a break-in and double homicide? She wouldn't even have needed to cross the road. She was dealing with a truly inconsiderate killer.

This raised another interesting problem, now she thought about it. The front door to Buscemi's first floor flat above the *Spice of Night* restaurant was just a short distance away along the small parade of shops, maybe fifty feet. But the uniformed plod standing in front of *Bohemia* was doubtless still watching the Met's newest recruit, and while she was hardly Batman now she had a shiny badge and everything, she still didn't feel comfortable with the flatfoots knowing where she lived, like some sort of normal detective. They might start calling around with fresh cases, treating her, South West London's premier feline sleuth, like *staff*.

Well, why not take the more picturesque route home after all? She sauntered to the right, sticking close against the brick wall as the traffic continued to rattle down Castelnau with what seemed to her to be an unnecessary amount of noise and fuss.

When the junction with Trinity Church Road came up

on her left, after a very unreasonable ten yards or so, she wrapped herself round it, purring with contentment. No one knew these streets better than her, no one.

In a few moments, she'd hopped up on to the roof of a Nissa Micra, jumped to a low wall, climbed up to a slightly higher wall, and was on the flat roof wasteland that led to her flat's back door.

Buscemi trotted along the flat roofs behind the parade of shops, her agile mind spinning with conjecture. Half a dozen hypotheses were formulated and discarded before the voices below her managed to impinge on her thoughts.

"Disparu? C'est-a-dire quoi, disparu?"

"Je sais pas! C'etait la, sur les tomates!"

"Quoi, donc? Nous avons un voleur?"

Buscemi froze. Her staff had some sort of history with languages, and they still watched the occasional film full of earnest foreign gibberish and people on beaches looking miserable. She dimly remembered '*voleur*' as being foreign for 'thief'. Or some sort of cloth. As a crime-solving cat with a taste for shredding curtain fabric, it was all very relevant, either way.

She looked over the wall into the small yard at the back of *Spoonful,* the French café. Two angry faces stared back up at her.

'*Le petit chat?*' one of them asked the other.

'*Non, les chats mangent pas d'ail. Les vollailles, peut-être, hein?*'

Buscemi could tell the second speaker was the boss from the tangible reluctance with which the first speaker laughed dutifully at what was apparently a joke.

Break-ins, squirrelcide, *and* possible cloth theft. She was building up an impressive caseload on her first day with the badge. Buscemi continued trotting over the rooftops. She'd learned a long time ago not to maintain eye contact with humans while she was busy thinking. It made them feel uncomfortable, and they started watching what they said around her – no, her anonymity was her greatest interrogation tool, given she couldn't seem to reliably speak to the bipedal lunks.

She hopped over a low wall, and picked up speed as she dashed across one last expanse of flat roofs, studded with solar panels and skylights, before she squeezed through the railings of her flat's 'balcony'. It was really just a fence that someone had erected to partition off a corner of the roof next to the back door. The world's cheapest garden furniture was piled in a mouldering heap in one corner, next to a plant pot full of mud and rainwater, and the chunky extractor fan that regularly carried enticing cooking smells from the kitchens of *Spice of Night*, directly below.

And a small golden-coloured cocker spaniel puppy. Buscemi skidded to a half as she noticed the wretched snuffling thing, pawing at an old broom with game determination as it tried to chew the bristles.

"Oh, great. Puddles."

At the sound of her voice, the puppy swung round, over-balancing in the process and sprawling on all fours, its long russet ears settling like a blanket over its forepaws.

"Hinn..." it whined, before its tail began to wag.

"It's been two weeks, how are they not fed up with you yet?" Buscemi wondered. "The sandwich toaster only lasted three days, and they never even bothered to take the DVD recorder out of its box."

"Buscemi! Come inside! Come on, ignore this silly monster – he's nothing to be afraid of." Scruffy Staff was standing in the doorway in pajamas and a blue dressing gown, holding a steaming mug of coffee. He was clearly reluctant to venture out on to the balcony in his bare feet.

"Hurruff!" The puppy's affronted yelp was so pathetic that Buscemi would have laughed, if she'd been the sort of cat who ever cracked a smile.

She stared the dog down as she replied. "I'm only afraid of getting the wretched thing's poo under my claws. Couldn't you at least get one that came pre-fitted with a cork?"

The creature's vacantly wide green eyes took on an almost affronted expression for a moment, before its features relaxed and a dark puddle began spreading on the asphalt and gravel beneath its paws.

"Good boy," Scruffy Staff cooed. "He's learning to wee outside, Buscemi. Isn't he clever?"

"I think you need to re-evaluate your standards," Buscemi replied. "Outside's a pretty big target, kind of hard to miss, and he's *still* managing to piddle on his own paws. By the time I was his age, I could hit a twelve inch tray every time, *and* shovel the litter all over the carpet so you knew it was time to change it. You're welcome, by the way."

Scruffy Staff scooped up the puppy awkwardly in his free hand, trying to hide a grimace as it scrabbled at his moderately clean dressing gown with wee-sodden paws. "Come on, silly cat. It's freezing out here."

Buscemi turned her tail with a medium flounce, and slunk off towards the old mattress that lay mouldering next to the skylight on the Indian restaurant's roof. She could have a proper think, while staying within sight of the staff and making sure they got the message that she was a bit cheesed off about the whole dumb animal situation.

The lumpy grey plains of her flat roof kingdom were hypnotic. She could stare at the skylights and extractor fans on the distant horizon of China Express's roof, or she could zoom in on the tiny packed gravel pebbles at her paws, flecked with dust, muck, lichen and woodlice. It was a great way to recalibrate.

She had a body, an ID, and a vague time of death. She had no motive, no murder weapon, no obvious suspects. Where should she focus her efforts? Where should she even *start*? She needed more data, but in a city this size, the data was overwhelming. How could a little black cat possibly be expected to know what was relevant and what was just noise?

Behind her, Blonde Staff's worried voice rang out over

the rooftops. "Buscemi? We put the silly puppy in his bed in the kitchen and closed the door. You can come in now. Please."

Buscemi did a very small flounce, but her heart wasn't in it. She needn't let this responsibility overwhelm her, not when she had certain resources she could call on. Yes, she could make it all someone else's problem to get started on all the boring thinking stuff, and then she could tie it all up and take all the credit. Probably get a promotion as well!

Of course! She was going at this whole detective thing all wrong. Sure, she could wander around poking her nose into complex relationships, raking up old dirt, and rattling skeletons in closets, but there was an old cat proverb...

She who digs through dusty litter, reaps only stale turds. In other words, why risk putting her adorable little nose to the grindstone when she could just get other people to do all the dirty work for her?

Murder might be a bit beyond her immediate social circle, but it wasn't as though she was unconnected. She'd long known who, in theory, you needed to speak to if you wanted to uncover the odd secret, the power behind the curtain in this suburb. But they were not the kind of people you approached lightly, so she'd never had the opportunity to make their acquaintance. She just had to work out the best way to approach them.

Buscemi twitched her tail in a suddenly decisive fashion. She'd go first thing tomorrow, after her two mid-morning naps and her daily lying-around training. Lunchtime. She'd go at the crack of lunchtime.

Maybe at the crack of a continental lunchtime.

Having taken this important decision, Buscemi decided to wander back inside the flat and show the staff that she was not ungracious. She looked around briefly for a small mouse or baby bird to take in, because arriving for dinner without a gift for your host is thoroughly bad manners, but after she saw nothing obvious on the roof, she resolved to merely purr at the staff until they felt special and valued.

Suckers.

She sauntered into the living room, weaving between the legs of the glass dining table that was just a little too big for the room, and sniffing at the mishmash of film posters and vintage magazine covers that were hanging in frames along the length of one wall.

Both the staff were putting on their shoes and coats, which stopped her in her tracks for a moment. This wasn't the time for them to go to work! It was the time for them to sit and give her attention until she got bored and wandered off. How dare they abandon her like this?

"He's still so young, are you sure he'll be OK?" Blonde Staff asked, as the scruffy one took a long coiled lead from where it had been hanging from the door handle.

"He'll be fine, you know what people are like. They'll queue up to fuss over him, and it'll give us a nice break to have a few beers."

"You said *one* beer!"

"I say a lot of things."

And in a whirlwind of giggling and excited yapping, the three of them were gone. Buscemi licked her paw in thought as she heard them thumping down the stairs, and hissed softly as she heard the front door slam behind them as they spilled out on Castelnau.

"I hope you have a really rotten time," Buscemi mewed after them, softly. She'd heard of this sort of thing happening with other, less adorable cats, but she had such a pretty nose and had paid her way in the flat. Until the staff had suddenly started acting as though they were above all of that sort of thing, she'd brought all sorts of exciting and nearly dead rodents to the balcony door.

She swished her tail. It would pass. Scruffy Staff had been with her since she'd been a kitten, and if the worst came to the worst, Puddles would grow old and die while she was still in her prime. Pretty black cats have a slightly lateral approach to positive mental attitude, but that kind of reasoning never failed to put an extra happy gloss on her sleek black fur. Buscemi sat down on her haunches with her tail arranged delicately around her, and considered her case, and what a clever and magnificent cat she would be once she'd solved it.

Where had it come from, this compulsion for justice? This urge to solve crimes, wherever she found them, and whatever form they took? It was a question that Buscemi considered from time to time, and she reflected on it now, as she basked in the warmth of the electric heater that sat next to the rug in the living room. She knew becoming a detective was an ambition of hers that stretched back to the earliest months of her fourteen years, the initial impulse lost in the mists of her earliest memory.

This much she knew, though. Buscemi had never cared much for other cats, on the whole, but she'd never yet met one as driven to unravel mysteries, and to right wrongs, as she was. The other cats of her limited acquaintance seemed mostly content to sit on cushions, snooze, and lie in wait under parked cars in order to kill small creatures.

As chance would have it those were all Buscemi's favourite things to do as well, but they were all activities that gave her nimble mind a lot of time to observe, reflect, make connections, and draw conclusions.

After she'd heard her Staff grumbling about what was eating Blonde Staff's tomatoes during the night, she'd been bored enough to look into it. She'd observed that only a small bird would have been able to balance on the delicate plant in order to peck at the upper-most fruit. Probably something about the size of a sparrow.

So she went out and maimed the first sparrow she saw, and deposited the terrified bird on the kitchen floor just as Scruffy Staff was making the coffee one morning.

They hadn't seemed too delighted, but Buscemi had concluded from this that they'd been unable to follow her deductive reasoning and therefore questioned her conclusions. From that moment she resolved, until such time as she'd worked out how to file a report that humans could read, to keep the summary justice element of her investigative life well away from the staff's bleeding hearts. The sweet summer children.

But she knew they understood her passion. As she roamed the flat roof one evening, ears twitching as each car and dog walker drifted down Methyr Terrace, she'd heard Blonde Staff laugh.

"She walks as though she thinks she's a panther!"

"She's investigating everything," Scruffy Staff had replied.

And from that moment she'd known she was on the right path, when even her Staff could see her destiny, even if they didn't quite understand it.

***

Much later, Buscemi woke from her snooze with a start, as she heard the stupid dog bounding down the hallway, and darted into her sanctuary under the sofa. The idiot creature hadn't yet worked out that it was easily small enough to follow her, and as long as she swiped at his snuffling nose every so often, he'd get the message eventually and go and chew the ottoman instead.

From her shelter, she could hear the staff moving around in the puppy's wake. It was dark outside, and they were stumbling more than usual, but the giggling was about normal. She gave a frosty little sniff as she deduced they'd been in the pub all this time, and felt a rare twinge of jealousy when she realised that Puddles had obviously been allowed to go with them. Not that she'd be seen dead going for walks on a lead, but it would have been nice to be asked, she reflected. There must have been something really good about that pub, considering the amount of time they spent in it. There must have been *loads* of cushions. Buscemi liked cushions.

"I can't believe you really took it!" Scruffy Staff was giggling loudest as he switched on the television. There was a late film on, and Arnold Schwarzenegger was breaking into a large house. "We actually nicked a statue!"

"We didn't nick it!" Blonde Staff sounded indignant, but was still giggling.

"Yes, we did! From an actual charity shop!"

"It was *outside* the charity shop! There's even a sign *telling* people not to leave stuff there."

"Yeah, it says 'don't leave donations outside the shop when we are closed, because drunk people might steal them.'"

"You're so boring! Anyway, it's cool."

"It's really not, it's hideous. You're a magpie for free stuff!"

"That's not true. I'll put puppy to bed now."

Blonde Staff's footsteps moved away to the kitchen, accompanied by her giggling and Puddles's permanently excited whimpering. Buscemi flinched as a heavy weight descended on the sofa and the cushions bulged down over her head.

She slunk out, and sure enough, Scruffy Staff had collapsed into the middle of the sofa, still giggling softly in the darkened living room.

"Look what the *dog* dragged in," she said with a sniff.

Scruffy Staff looked down at her with a vague frown. "I didn't realise you were in, Buscemi! Look at the monstrosity your mummy nicked from the charity shop!"

"It's not a monstrosity," Blonde Staff called from the kitchen, just as Buscemi yowled, "she's not my mummy." But she looked over anyway. It was a doorstop in the shape of an owl perched on a log. The thing was sitting in front of the sofa. It was about twice Buscemi's size, sculpted from grey plastic and given a highly rudimentary paint job. Its head looked to have been screwed on separately so it could be rotated, and two amber glass eyes stared at Buscemi in silent accusation.

Buscemi was distracted by the television as Arnie said "*encore d'ail*". She glanced at the screen where a subtitle read, "This needs more garlic". So someone had stolen a cafe's *garlic*? She supposed they must have done. After all, Arnold Schwarzenegger's deductive reasoning and grasp of modern languages was beyond reproach. *Interesting.*

Scruffy Staff cast a conspiratorial glance towards the kitchen, and lowered his voice. "I don't know what the hell she was thinking when she pinched that owl," he confided, "but I'm *totally* going to freak her out by moving its head slightly each night when she's not looking."

He hauled himself up from the sofa, and plonked the owl next to the TV, while Buscemi reflected he was on to a good wheeze. She resolved to freak *both of them* out by moving its head *again* each night when neither of them was looking. You had to keep the staff on their toes.

She strolled over to the ragged carrier bag it had presumably arrived in, to see if anyone had thought to put some treats for her inside it. Amazingly, just for once...

"Earthworms?" she said. "Guys, you shouldn't have. But I'm glad you did." She poked her head inside the bag, rooting deep in the clammy interior to reach the Gordian knot of dead worms at the bottom.

"Buscemi? What are you doing?" Scruffy Staff bounded across the floor and pulled her head from the carrier bag by her sparkly collar. She fumed at this vulgar treatment, but the idiot had already turned away and was yelling toward the kitchen.

"Ew! Have you seen the state of this bag? There's a pile of dead wildlife clagging up the bottom. You pinched a tramp's spring cleaning."

Blonde Staff swept back into the living room, and cast a disdainful glance at the bag. "Then it was very kind of the tramp to think of the hospice charity shop. Now, throw it in the bin, wash your hands, and let's have Doritos and ice creams in bed."

Buscemi exchanged a glance with the scruffy one, and hopped on to the balcony before he could close the door.

Outside, a jet droned low over the rooftops, its green

wing-lights cutting a swathe through the cloudless night sky, on its way to land at Heathrow. Buscemi gazed up at it as she rubbed her chin against a rusty green watering can. *Big floating bastard.*

It was moving deceptively slowly, however, and she found herself starting to think laterally. She hated that. Flashes of insight were a symptom of a chronically lazy detective, in her view. Having spent endless Sunday afternoons enduring the staff's compulsive viewing of ITV3 crime solving, she maintained that the presence of a locked room mystery just meant you hadn't looked hard enough for the key in the first place.

But those planes seemed to drift overhead twice a minute all day long. They seemed random enough to her, with their array of paint jobs, and the many directions in which they peeled off after they'd climbed high into the air, but presumably there was some kind of order to it all? Could a killer hitch a ride on one of those sleek silver geese, and then drop on to the roof?

She licked her lips in irritation. *No.* Humans were rubbish at jumping off things without squishing at the best of times, and those jets looked higher up than even she would want to chance. Maybe a whole fifty feet!

So the murderer couldn't have jumped from a jet. But as she gazed out over the allotments on Trinity Church Road, Buscemi couldn't shake one unsettling phrase from her mind.

Death from above.

2 THE BARNES-WIDE WEB

The sun's first feeble rays crawled across the living room to the saggy spot on the sofa where Buscemi had spent the night. On any normal day, this would be her cue to throw a weary velvet paw over her eyes and roll over until there was some food.

This morning, however, she'd been awake for hours. Driven from her sleep by a vague but palpable sense of unease, that gnawed at her subconscious like a ball of silver foil just out of paw's reach under the bed.

What was she missing? Flollops the squirrel, the theft, whether it was garlic or cloth? She couldn't help thinking there was a missing piece to the puzzle; that she was overlooking something fundamentally obvious, something right in front of her...

The chimes of her staff's alarm rang distantly from their quarters. She heard the scruffy staff silence his phone, but Buscemi's train of thought was already derailed.

No matter, she would go and recline on the servants' bed, while they stroked and pampered her as befitted her splendour. It was an honour that she bestowed on her retinue from time to time, and it never failed to focus her concentration on the matter at hand.

She stood up and stretched, arching her spine to its limits, and grimacing at the owl thing. "They'd better have good chin-rubbing nails this morning, this is a tough one," she purred at the doorstop's glazed amber eyes.

A soft whimpering sounded from the kitchen. "Hinnn... hinnn..." Buscemi glowered at the closed kitchen door, willing the brute to stay silent, just this one day.

It was too late. "Hinnn... Urf-urg! Urg-urg!"

"I suppose I'd better take him out," groaned the scruffy one over the gentle rustle of sheets, his voice thick with sleep.

"Just put him on the balcony for a bit, honey bunny," the blonde one replied. "He can come up on the bed once he's... you know..."

Buscemi gave a low growl and settled back down. She pretended not to hear the joyful squeaky barking when the scruffy one opened the kitchen door to unleash the beast, and by the time the two of them scuffed past the sofa, she was so convincingly asleep that Scruffy Staff didn't even pause to scratch her ears. The Judas.

She heard the balcony door open, and was readying herself for a really satisfying sustained sulk, when the scruffy one started bleating again.

"What the – Eccleston, no!"

"Hinn... hinn... hurrup! Hurrup!"

"Get away from that! Come here! Good boy!"

Buscemi flexed her claws as her train of thought plunged into the chasm of daily dog-related anarchy. She tried to relax. She was missing something, but she felt it wasn't anything she was going to untangle in a flash of deductive reasoning. She needed more data. She desperately wanted to say 'more clues' but couldn't face her own disapproval, she knew how scathing she could be.

"What's wrong?" Blonde Staff was making her way down the hallway, fastening her dressing gown.

"The bloody cat's dumped a dead blue tit by the door! Eccleston's trying to do the autopsy face-first, if you know what I mean?"

Buscemi chose to ignore certain portions of that statement. Luckily the blonde one was sharp enough to defend the detective's honour. "Buscemi's been indoors all night, remember? The stupid bird just flew into the window. Look, you can see where it splatted on the glass, poor thing."

Sure enough, there was an imprint of a bird, wings spread, smeared across the window like a ghostly chalk outline. Blonde Staff went up a fraction of a notch in Buscemi's estimation, the silhouette was hardly easy to see.

"All right, well done Miss Marple," moaned the scruffy one. "Now can you help me stop our dog from eating the evidence?"

Buscemi rose stiffly and made her way to the back door. It was time to put her plans into motion, and to alert her ingenious network of contacts. And maybe to sit under a hedge for a couple of hours, she'd see if she still had the energy.

***

A little later, after being terribly busy and important for a couple of hours, Buscemi sat on a low garden wall, facing *Bohemia* over the street. Ard 'Ren the fox was curled up next to her, trying vaguely to look like a ginger tom. They watched as the people of Barnes shuffled in and out of the cafe in their dozens, all of them pretending they had no interest in tawdry gossip.

"They're open again already," Buscemi said, "just as I predicted."

Ard 'Ren yawned, covering her mouth daintily with the white tip of her bushy tail. "You're a genius. Are you really going to look into this stupid squirrel business?"

There was a long pause as traffic swished past. Buscemi was giving the question her full attention.

"Yes, I think so," she said at length. "A human asked

me. Even if he is a hipster alcoholic, that's quite a coup just for bragging rights. And… well, it's Flollops. We all *knew* Flollops, even if he was a bit weird. He was one of us."

Ard 'Ren nodded, her eyes on one of the banana peels that unaccountably littered the pavements of Castelnau. "Did you do it, then?"

"No! Actually. And *I'm* the detective here. I should be asking that."

"Sorry."

"You're all right. Did *you* do it?"

Ard 'Ren frowned. "Dunno. Which one was Flollops?"

"Twitchy-looking. Kept doing that weird Alastair MacGowan impersonation, and claiming it was 'meta'. Even that time Alastair was actually in the pub garden staring right at us."

"Oh! *Him*! No, dear, dumb animals are one thing, but that poor creature was just *disturbed*."

Buscemi narrowed her eyes. "Yeah, that's what I thought. Flollops was a bit mental, but beyond harmless. You'd have to be a proper headcase to want to off him, and then to not even bother eating the evidence?"

"Unless he saw something he shouldn't? Knew too much?"

"Like what? He just used to sit up that scrubby tree of his by the estate agent, trying to claw his eyes out with his own tail."

"So maybe it's to do with the other murder? That human?"

Buscemi shook her head emphatically. "No. No one desperate enough to kill a squirrel on *my* patch is going to worry about some boring human."

"So you've no idea, really," said 'Ard Ren, stifling a yawn.

Buscemi bristled a bit at this, but not much, just in case the fox took offence. Their interspecies *entente cordiale* sometimes seemed like a brittle arrangement, and the clever little cat had no intention of testing its boundaries, especially given that Ren was the one creature in SW13 that could conceivably take her in a scrap.

She gave her tail a lofty swish. "I'm looking for an angle," she admitted. "So I sent out the Inedibles. I'm expecting word back any moment."

"Grasses and stool pigeons," Ren gave a dismissive sniff. "You'll need to improve your network now you're *official*."

"Improve? How?"

"An actual pigeon would be a good start," said Ren, "with or without a stool. Aerial surveillance, and that."

A shadow swept over the two animals for a moment, and Buscemi shivered. "I don't know, Ren. I never trust anything so stupid it craps on its own feet."

Which was when a tiny voice piped up from their feet. "I throw my poo."

Apparently having appeared from nowhere, a fluffy grey hamster was sitting in the grass between them, twitching its whiskers primly.

"See, Ren? Sean here throws his poo. So trust his evidence... but never let him make you a salad."

With a flurry of squeaks and chirps, the Inedibles emerged from the long grass, and formed two surprisingly neat rows in front of Buscemi and 'Ard Ren. A motley collection of frogs, mice, hedgehogs, and even the odd small rat. All scuffed up, tousled, or missing the odd limb. All of them creatures that for various reasons, including not being hungry or having some sleeping to do, Buscemi had spared over the years, and classified as Inedible. In return for their eternal gratitude and vigilance. In that order.

Sean the Zombie Hamster was their de facto leader, a three year old Syrian who, legend had it, had crawled from his grave beneath a rose bush during a recent Barnes medical emergency, and consequently declared himself immortal.

His story struck Buscemi as somewhat unlikely, but she admired his brazen disregard for anything so mundane as the truth.

She mewed softly now, to make sure she had their attention. And then she purred just one single word. "Clues."

There was a brief susurration of animal chatter as they decided on a running order. Finally a three-legged mouse stumbled forward. "Whole lotta birds crashing in windows, guv."

Buscemi shook her head as 'Ard Ren snickered next to her. "Still getting those phantom pains from the old missing forepaw, Basil?"

"Er… when it's damp, guv. Sometimes."

The kitten detective flexed her own forepaw, claws popping out. "Want something to take whatever passes for your mind off it?"

Quailing before the icy cat and the amused fox, Basil's teeth began to chatter in panic. "*Lotta* birds, though, guv," he implored. "*Loads*. And just hitting the same three or four windows, all down Lonsdale Road."

Buscemi put down her paw, apparently mollified. "That's quite a good *fact*," she acknowledged. "But it's not a Clue. Still, give Ren the addresses, she could probably use a snack. Anything else?"

Sean gave an important cough. "Weed!"

"My dear fellow, we all have to answer the odd call of nature, even if we don't all choose to throw it around afterwards."

"No, I mean… *weeds*. I saw a bloke wandering around the churchyard, poking through the grass near the hedge."

Basil chipped in, nodding excitedly. "Ubiquitous Terry saw him out the back of Harrods Village. And then I saw him hop over the wall into the garden on the end of Trinity Church Passage. Just wandering around every bit of long grass, poking through it and nodding."

'Ard Ren swished her tail. "A *bloke* hopped over that

wall? It's a high wall."

"Right you are, guv," agreed the hamster in the cheery tones of a small creature that would have had trouble climbing over a beer bottle.

There was a pause as Buscemi considered the reports. "So let me see if I understand correctly," she said with an icy calm that made all the Inedibles except Basil shrink back nervously. "I send you out to gather information on curious goings-on in Barnes, and the very best you can do is to note a rise in the number of clumsy birds... and an itinerant grass enthusiast?"

"*Weeds*," Basil corrected her, bravely. "He's not just poking about in grass, it's any weeds."

"I don't care, I'm investigating a squirrelcide! And right now I have a feeling that some other crime-solving cat might soon be investigating half a dozen mouseycides! I'm a very clever detective, actually, but I can't solve crimes without any leads – come back in a couple of days, and you'd better have something tangible for me, or you're all officially becoming Edible again. Get out of my sight."

The cluster of animals dispersed in a heartbeat, though 'Ard Ren's eyes flashed with amusement as her keen ears picked up the mice all asking each other what 'tangible' meant.

***

"Urf, urf," the dog slobbered in Buscemi's direction while she stretched and stared out of the window with disdain.

One of her staff giggled from the sofa. "She's still grumpy about puppy. Bet they'll be best friends in a month."

Buscemi gave a little shudder, and started licking her velvety paws to hide it. Friends with an incontinent four-legged mop? Who did they think she was?

"Let's just hope she doesn't teach him any of her

naughty little tricks." The other member of staff, the scruffy one, was looking surprisingly serious for once. Perhaps he was even sober. Blimey.

"What do you mean?"

"The spiders were one thing, but I shifted the owl earlier when I was doing the hoovering. I found another dead blue tit. I think she's been hunting again."

Midway through cleaning her right forepaw, Buscemi froze and felt her heart swell with pride in spite of herself. She'd barely had *time* to hunt for weeks, but she was touched by the regard her staff clearly had for her deadly prowess.

Blonde Staff giggled again. "Don't be silly! She's too chubby!"

Buscemi narrowed her eyes and tried to remember which was Blonde Staff's favourite pair of shoes. It was in for some serious pooing. Anyway, she was all muscle. And big-boned. And it was glandular. Or something.

The other one barely helped. "I know, right? But inside the living room? How else did it get there? I think we ought to get her a new collar. With a bell." He kept his voice low, and tried not to meet Buscemi's implacable gaze. *Kiss-arse.*

"Oh no! She always jingles round the place like a Morris dancer with an itchy bum!"

Scruffy Staff sighed. "Yeah, fair point. OK. But we'll keep an eye out. Ooh, Columbo's on!"

As the staff sank into their usual catatonic trance opposite the television, Buscemi wrinkled her pretty nose. Bells and collars, was it? The hell with *that*. Still, she knew she wasn't hunting, so the problem would go away on its own.

"Urf, urf!"

Buscemi glanced down idly to watch the puppy's fresh attempt to climb up to the windowsill, its paws stretching to the armchair's cushion. It caught her gaze, and dropped to the floor, wagging its tail excitedly. And then it wet itself on the floor.

As the staff surfaced from their trance with a chorus of groans and reached for the mop they kept on standby for just this purpose, Buscemi reflected that at least they'd been distracted from thoughts of bells and collars.

"Cheers, Puddles," she muttered grudgingly.

***

It was a cold, grey morning, and the staff had been surprised how keen Buscemi was for them to open the door so she could get out on to the flat roofs and start her day's crime-solving. She had hung around staring at skylights for a few minutes, until she was sure they'd both gone to work. There would be nothing more embarrassing than bumping into the staff while she was *conducting her enquiries*.

She headed north, towards the river, scurrying along the pavement, and jumping into the front gardens of Castlenau Mansions as soon as she could, away from the crowds thronging the pavements to catch the scarce buses that crawled across Hammersmith Bridge, one at a time.

Finally, she shot across the junction with Riverview Gardens, and miaowed with satisfaction as the bulky green bridge filled her field of vision, stretching into the distance across the River Thames.

As Buscemi scampered down the uneven concrete ramp next to the bridge, she cast nervous glances around her. She'd been this way before, of course, but only in hot pursuit of a particularly tasty suspect. Strictly speaking, she was out of her territory, and she just had to hope her trespass went unnoticed.

The ramp quickly led to the Thames Path, a broad tree-lined footpath with luxury flats on one side, and the swollen expanse of the Thames on the other. Buscemi looked longingly at the shadows where the path ran left under Hammersmith Bridge itself. But she pressed on to the right, dodging a fat cyclist in screaming lycra as she crossed the path, and slunk low in the tall grass and nettles that bordered the steep stone bank down to the water's edge.

Hunkered down overlooking the lapping waters, Buscemi tried to ignore the over-energetic rowers carving their way through the grey dawn waters. Instead she scanned the narrow shoreline of sludgy pebbled beach, at which the slowly rising tidal waters were sucking greedily. He *had* to be there, somewhere. And, suddenly, there he was.

"I require assistance," Buscemi yowled over to the Deathless Guardian of Hammersmith Bridge.

The heron didn't even bother to turn his crested head, but continued to stare downstream as he posed regally in the shallows under the bridge. Ducks and coots bobbed around him, but never quite close enough, through coincidence or self-preservation, to jostle or even trouble the noble bird's vigil.

"A cat 'requires assistance'! Just hark at that!" the heron mused. "Away wi' thee, tha great dunnock."

Buscemi shuffled back a little on her paws. "You are the Guardian of this Bridge?"

The heron deigned to swing its long beak in Buscemi's direction, and she did her utmost not to quail under its beady gaze. It lifted one leg out of the shallows in a suitably considered and stately fashion. "Oh, aye, I'm the Guardian. Fated to an endless vigil over this ancient crossing. Ever since my predecessor fell to a stray oar in the 1870 Boat Race. But do I look daft enough to run around doing a cat's bidding? Do I 'eck as like! What do you think I am? Human? Try scratching at my front door for a few hours and see what happens. The cloth-bags might fall for it, but an animal that craps in a box is still an animal, for all that."

"Should I try Barnes Bridge then, perhaps?" Buscemi asked, a trifle acidly.

"Aye. Sling yer hook." The heron bobbed its head.

Buscemi stood, uncurling her tail with a flourish. "Fine. I'm sure the police will understand how busy you are."

"Police?"

Buscemi tossed her head as she turned back towards the ramp. "I'm assisting them with a murder enquiry. Perhaps you've heard of Detective Buscemi Daintypaws?"

The heron planted both feet in the water as it turned to face Buscemi squarely. "The mental moggy that holds kangaroo courts for rats, behind China Express? That's you? You're *famous*."

Cats aren't very good at blushing, from a biological point of view. Luckily they're also not generally inclined to feeling embarrassed particularly often. Buscemi tilted her head slightly, and worried whether even that reaction might suggest she was going soft in her old age.

"I solve crimes, Mr Heron. It's in my blood."

"Crimes? Snaffled Twixes was what I heard."

"Yes, well. Look after the details, and the bigger picture tends to take care of itself. My caseload leans towards confectionery theft and unauthorised pooing, true, but as a result I think you'll find it's been *months* since a kingpin smuggled a miniature nuclear warhead through *my* patch. Disturbed cyborg veterans of galactic wars just *know better* than to leave a trail of hideously disfigured corpses in their bloody wake when they pass through Castelnau Court. It's been simply *ages* since I had to play a game of psychological cat-and-mouse with a serial killer who kept trying to convince me that we weren't so very different. Mind you, the last one actually *was* a mouse, so it wasn't the most challenging nemesis I've ever had."

The heron beat its wings, just once, gracefully. It did everything gracefully. "I've heard enough. Please, tell me how I can help you go away."

"You're the Guardian of Hammersmith Bridge. I have a case. I need to share evidence with, and warn, the proper authorities in Putney. Maybe Chiswick too. This is big."

The heron and the cat both looked up as a sudden squawk rang out over the swollen river. A shabby mallard drake fell from the sky, quacking all the way. At the last moment, he managed to pull out of his nose dive and scrambled a few feet to the right, building just enough momentum to plough a turbulent furrow in the sluggish water.

The duck had somehow landed upside down, and his vivid yellow legs flailed pointlessly at the air for a few moments before he righted himself. The drake bobbed in the water for about a minute, until he judged that everyone had forgotten about his dramatic arrival, then swam over to join the heron.

"Yo, Stan."

"Morning, Drake. Drunken flying again? That was a hell of a splashdown."

"Chill, Daft Wader. I'm fly, dig? Got the moves." Drake threw back his head, stuck out his vivid yellow bill and made a spirited attempt at moonwalking, which is shockingly unimpressive when you're bobbing up and down in a murky river with your legs underwater. "Got. The. *Moves*."

Buscemi blinked. "What on earth are you talking about, ducky?"

As quickly as the river's eddies would allow, Drake swung round to face the little black cat. "Who's the furjob?" he hissed at Stanley.

The heron rolled his eyes. "Oh God, I can't believe I'm saying this. Drake, meet Detective Buscemi Daintypaws."

Buscemi frowned. "Twinklefur."

"Eh?"

"My name is Detective Buscemi Daintypaws Twinklefur, and I have a message for you."

Drake cocked his head to one side. "What message is that?"

Shivering in the chill wind that whistled along the river's flat expanse, Buscemi leaned as far over the bank as she could, and kept her voice low. "Watch the weeds."

Stanley took a majestic step forward, and jutted his long beak toward the little black cat. "Is that supposed to make any sense?"

Drake was sniggering until Buscemi spoke again. Her emerald green eyes were wide, pleading. Her soft voice insistent. "Please? OK, for now it's a hunch. But I think it's an informed hunch. Watch the weeds. If I'm right, it'll be obvious when you see what I'm looking for.

Drake spun in a circle with a derisive quack. "Stan, you gotta talk to the Council, transfer bridges. These Barnes furjobs... they're jokes, man. They're all pure jokes."

Still staring into Buscemi's face, Stanley hadn't moved. Though to be fair that was far from unusual. Several drops of water dripped from his tail feathers before the stately heron raised his streamlined head to stare at Hammersmith Bridge's broad green arches, deep in thought.

Eventually, he nodded. "You've got your message, Drake."

"Wha?" Drake beat his wings and honked his disbelief at the top of his voice, prompting a tight gaggle of Canada geese to glower over in their direction from a clump of bushes a hundred yards downstream.

"You're kidding, Stan? This furjob's way cray like Tay Tay. This is pure whack, man."

Stanley swung his beak to point down at the duck. By his languid standards it was a sharp gesture, and the mallard fell silent immediately.

"You have your message. Get down to David at Putney Bridge first, then back up to Derek at Barnes Bridge and then Chiswick, via the Wetland Centre and Duke's Meadows."

Drake beat his wings again. "That's gonna take all morning! I had some seriously tranquil bobbing up and down to do today. All that weed's going to get tangled up on some cormorant or something who doesn't even appreciate it properly. Man."

Stanley and Buscemi just stared at him, until finally Drake fluffed up his chest feathers and drew in his beak.

"Fine, whatever. This is whack..."

Still grumbling, the duck beat his wings, surged forward in the water, and slowly climbed into the air. Suddenly Drake was flying, a long-necked streak of colour, ready to spread Buscemi's message along the Thames.

As he flew, he grumbled. "Man, this is whack... whack! Whack! Whack! Whack!"

As the truculent duck sped towards Fulham FC's Craven Cottage stadium, his wails of protest faded and were buried under the gentle but persistent sound of lapping water and heavy traffic passing over the rickety bridge.

It was Buscemi who broke the comparative silence first. "At least now I know why herons are so into Tai Chi."

Stanley shuffled on to his other foot. "Look, he's a good lad, OK? What is all this? Is there anything I ought to be worrying about?"

A lesser cat would have quailed under his piercing stare, and even Buscemi was tempted to look away. "I don't know. A dead squirrel, killed by persons unknown and I swear I never did it, OK? He was a good squirrel, he used to annoy people that I didn't like much. Oh yes, and there was some dead human on the floor too. It's important enough that humans have called in a cat detective. I think that might mean it's the most serious thing that's ever happened."

Stanley made an odd noise at that point, and Buscemi thought he probably had something caught in his throat. Which must be something that happened an awful lot, given the immense length of his neck, so she resolved not to mention it.

"But don't worry," she said in her best professionally reassuring voice. "I am on the case, and the law-abiding citizens of Barnes can rest easy."

***

As she slunk across the flat roofs, Buscemi's ears pricked up as she heard the rumble of multiple voices from her living room, interspersed with excited yelps from Puddles. That usually meant visitors.

Sure enough, as she slipped through the fence, she saw that the staff had been joined by Interim Staff, the lady that sometimes came to do her bidding while Scruffy and Blonde Staff were taking annual leave.

She'd have clawed her own face off rather than admit it, but in many ways she rather liked Interim Staff. Apparently she kept rats at home, which meant she smelled a little bit like food. She even seemed to have accepted a role as staff for the creatures, whose tails were so long that Buscemi couldn't help but think of them as tiny scurrying kebabs. It took all sorts. She also worked in theatres, and brought tales of various theatre cats. Buscemi liked a bit of showbiz gossip, and apparently there was one theatre where a cat slept in the box office. Now *that* was glamorous.

On the other paw, her appearance often heralded the disappearance of Blonde and Scruffy Staff for a lengthy trip to the nearest pub.

She prowled into the living room to greet Interim Staff, who was sitting on the sofa and quaffing an ambitiously vast glass of wine. Blonde and Scuffy Staff were similarly encumbered, and it boded well for them staying in the flat and not embarking on one of their drunken odysseys while leaving her to the tender and infinitely irritating mercies of Puddles, with no one to open the balcony door no matter how insistently she stared.

"Here's Buscemi!" Scruffy Staff said as she slunk in and scowled at them all, purring only grudgingly as Blonde Staff and Interim Staff tickled her ears.

"We'd better watch out," Blonde Staff said, giggling,

"she's been massacring the local wildlife."

"Uhuh," said Interim Staff. "Is that why you got the bird-scarer?"

The other two followed her gaze as she pointed at the owl statue in the corner.

"Is that what it is?" asked Scruffy Staff.

"Yeah, you see them on rooftops on some of the Castelnau mansions, probably to keep herons out of the ponds."

"Good luck with that," muttered Buscemi, remembering Stanley's steely glower.

Scruffy Staff stared hard at Blonde, who even had the decency to briefly look embarrassed.

"We found it," she tried.

"She nicked it," Scruffy Staff clarified. "From a charity shop."

"*Outside* a charity shop," Blonde Staff objected. "And we rent this flat, so really we're charity cases anyway. I think that's even the law in some cities."

"Not in Barnes," Scruffy Staff said with a certain gloomy relish. "They still transport children for stealing bread here. They transport them to Hammersmith rather than Australia, but it's the thought that counts."

Buscemi shuddered at the mention of Hammersmith. It was a shadowy realm that loomed over the far side of the river, full of tall buildings, construction sites, and pigeons so packed with testosterone that she was surprised they could even get in the air without stabbing themselves on their own beaks.

Blonde Staff changed the subject. "How did you become a world expert on bird scarers? Are you writing a play about them?"

Interim Staff laughed. "No, I found one too, in a skip outside my flat the other night. I put it opposite the rats, to freak them out."

They all laughed at that, even Buscemi, who liked the thought of reminding the rodents who was boss.

"Did it work?" asked Scruffy Staff.

She shook her head. "I don't think so. There was a cranefly with all its legs pulled off on top of its head this morning. They must have been climbing the thing. Still, it stopped Caryl Churchill from chewing her way into the boiler again."

There followed the usual conversation about how often Interim Staff let her rats roam freely in her flat. Buscemi didn't understand why anyone would be surprised, she was a very ethical cat, and fully approved of free range farming.

"Anyway," said Blonde Staff. "Buscemi's been at the bluetits, so we've got to get her a bell. You're getting one tomorrow, aren't you honey bunny?"

Scruffy Staff coughed, as Interim and Buscemi both giggled quietly at 'honey bunny'. He ran a hand through his hair. "Uh, yeah. When I next make it to the pet shop. Tomorrow. Or maybe Wednesday. Definitely soon."

He darted a guilty look at Buscemi. "Sorry, mate. It tolls for thee."

3 THE INEVITABLE AUTOPSY SCENE

The next morning, Stanley was not in a good mood. "You're not a maverick who breaks the rules but gets results, and you're not a wayward genius plagued by sudden flashes of insight. You're a little cat who's wasting my time with cryptic clues. Either tell me what you know, or sling your bleeding hook, all right?"

Wincing from the onslaught, Buscemi tried to keep calm, and scratched at her chin with a single claw. "So, nothing disturbed the weeds last night?"

"Of course nothing disturbed the blinkin' weeds last night!"

"Say it, don't spray it," Buscemi admonished the heron severely, but backed up when the ancient bird snarled at her through his sharp beak. "Look, this is where we are. We have a spate of garlic thefts, a dead squirrel, and now some wally's trying to frame me for some bluetit killings that I didn't even do. Though I could have if I'd wanted to. Easy. I'm lethal."

Buscemi trailed off, aware she'd lost her thread a little. "Um, did I forget anything?"

"Dead human," Stanley observed, taking a single stately sploshing step to the right as he spoke.

Buscemi shook her head in mild irritation. "Why does everyone keep banging on about him? He's not important, the human police do all that stuff anyway. I rubbed against their legs so hard they must have electrocuted themselves with static when they got back in their silly cars, but they wouldn't even show me their photos."

"Still, they're persistent bleeders," mused Stanley, deflating a little, "and he must have been involved. There must be some way to find out what the humans know."

"Ruff!" A raucous bark cut through the still air from the towpath. Buscemi's ears flattened against her head instinctively at the sound, but then she relaxed as she saw the distant dog and the man walking it.

"I think you may have something there, big bird. Catch you later."

She slunk back up the bank, and streaked through the thick undergrowth.

A few dozen yards towards Putney, she caught up with the dog. The huge black rottweiler, more bear than dog, sat on the path and stared dolefully at Buscemi while her owner stood behind her trying in vain to cajole her into moving.

She sighed. "It always comes down to shifting the old black dog. I never thought I'd say something so humiliating to a bum-sniffer, but here we are. I'm Detective Daintypaws, and I need your help."

Blinking slowly, the old dog slumped into a prone position. "Lola," she said ponderously. "Lola good girl."

It was Buscemi's turn to blink. "Um, yes, all right. I expect you are a good girl, probably. Now -"

"Good girl? Sausage roll?" Lola lumbered to her feet with a gently expectant light in her eyes.

"I... don't have a sausage roll. Look, there's been a murder in our area. You spend almost all your time on that section of Castelnau. Have you seen anything lately, out and about? Or... smelt anything? Anything unusual?"

"Yes."

"Well, what?"

"Sausage roll." Lola raised a plaintive paw and tried to plant it on Buscemi's shoulder. She took a step backwards, trying to keep it polite.

Buscemi sighed. "Well, you're consistent, I suppose. Could you at least keep an eye out?"

"Flollops is a distraction, an innocent bystander, stopping you from focusing on the real criminals at work in Barnes. You're a clever cat, not a policeman, so stop trying to think like one. You've not found a motive for the murder, even though you know everyone the victim knew. A policeman would dig deeper for a motive, but you know in your heart there *was* no motive. Flollops stumbled across something in *Bohemia*, and he died. The human had no business being in *Bohemia* either, and he died. Ergo, there was at least one more person in *Bohemia* that night, who was responsible for both their deaths. And what do you know about them?"

Buscemi reeled from the relentless outpouring of deductive reasoning that spilled languorously from the huge dog's old muzzle. Things she'd known deep down but not given sufficient weight in her enquiries. Leading her inescapably to conclusions she hadn't yet dared to contemplate.

"They're strong enough to kill a human while leaving no signs of physical struggle. And canny enough to know that even a maladjusted squirrel might prove to be a critical witness, when there's a crime-solving cat living less than half a block away."

Lola nodded wisely. "Sausage roll."

"I see. I've still got a lot to learn. It doesn't matter how, no offence, dogged I am in my tenacious pursuit of the truth, if I don't stop for long enough to ask the right questions."

Lola stared at Buscemi with huge, doleful eyes. And finally, the penny dropped.

"The right question. *How* did Flollops and the human

die?" she asked.

The old dog stood up, a little stiffly. She had no tail to speak of, but she looked very pleased with herself nonetheless.

"Lola good girl," she said, and lumbered away.

***

"Ah, my clever detective!" Cornetto spread his arms wide in greeting as Buscemi slunk through the door before it closed on the mother pushing five children in a single buggy. "Did you come to update your chief?"

Buscemi arched her back at the merest suggestion of such a pretty little cat ever having something so vulgar as a *boss*, but she forced down her proud reaction with effort. "You can't eat a chaffinch without swallowing a few feathers," to quote the ancient proverb she'd just made up.

"Actually, Mr Latteplease, I'm here to ask you a few more questions about the morning you discovered Flollops."

The embattled waiter smiled as Buscemi stared up at him, unblinking and all business. He bustled back behind the counter as his immense coffee machine steamed and clattered. In a wild flurry of elbows, he manipulated the chromed alchemical apparatus until its rattling reached an abrupt climax. He turned back, and was somehow holding a tiny cup of coffee between his thumb and forefinger.

"Perhaps it's not a report after all," he mused, "perhaps this is an interrogation? After all, where *was* I at the time of the killing, yes?"

He took a dainty slurp from his tinycino, and waggled his eyebrows at Buscemi over the rim of his thimble-sized cup. Was this absolute unit *flirting*? Had he not even heard of the #mewtoo movement? He probably thought it was a damn Pokémon or something.

"It would be very silly or extremely arrogant of you to deputise Castelnau's cleverest crime-solving cat to investigate a crime you'd committed yourself," Buscemi observed with the icy calm that she hoped one day would become her trademark. "No, I'm here because the briefing you gave me was woefully lacking in detail. What was the cause of death for Flollops Chez Arbre? Were you personally acquainted with the victim, and had you ever seen his Alastair McGowan impersonation? If it's not too much bother, what was the cause of death for that human? Because you said he'd been stabbed in a gang altercation before crawling in here to bleed out. Which doesn't explain how he got in here with no evidence of a break-in, why there were no reports of gang-related disturbances that evening - because I do only live fifty yards up the road, you know - and why there were no blood spatters visible on the pavement outside when I attended the scene the following morning."

Buscemi paused, struck by a sudden thought. "Or why I couldn't smell any fresh blood when I entered the place, now I come to think about it. You know what? Yes, this jolly well might be an interrogation. Why would you enlist a cat detective and then waste her time by feeding her false information?"

Cornetto sighed, and drained his cup. "Is a tough case, yes? I'm sorry, clever kitty. It's not easy, solving a simple crime in a complex world. Perhaps, you should take another look at the victim?"

"You still have Flollops here?" Buscemi tried not to come over too eager, aware she should have covered this stuff on that first fateful morning. "I thought he'd be paninis by now!"

The waiter tucked his empty cup under the counter, which he then wiped down with a flourish. After tossing the damp cleaning cloth over his shoulder, he pointed at Buscemi with a long, coffee-stained forefinger. "I show you. But don't you be eating any murder victims, clever cat."

The waiter strolled towards the back of the cafe and

Buscemi scampered after him, barely trying to disguise her excitement. It had taken her a while to adjust to the enormity of her responsibilities, but she'd got the size of it now, and she was about to do some proper CSI stuff!

As she scurried across the spot where the human had been lying, she had a quick sniff - one was all she needed - before she carried on, thoughtfully. She was sure they'd have given the floorboards a bit of a mopping before reopening *Bohemia*, but if someone had died a messy violent death on the floor, she'd expect to be able to smell some traces for at least a month or so. Odd.

A small door at the back of the cafe took Cornetto and Buscemi through a cramped stockroom and kitchen area. As they passed a cupboard full of bottles of red wine, Buscemi paused for a moment as she picked up an unexpected scent. She gave her sensitive and extremely pretty nose a quick lick in confusion, and sniffed again.

"Earthworms, in here?" she said. "Does this place get flooded or something?"

"Out here, clever cat!" Cornetto opened the back door, and daylight poured into the dingy kitchen.

Buscemi was so excited that she *almost* forgot to sit on the threshold and stare at the open door, while she weighed up the profound philosophical implications of choosing to go through it; she was desperate to dash through and get on with the Course of her Enquiries.

But she was a properly official crime-solving cat now, there was no excuse for being unprofessional. It wasn't as though Flollops was likely to be going anywhere, after all. So she sat and stared at the open doorway until Cornetto began to shift on his feet and to sigh quietly. Then she walked through, purring with satisfaction at a job well done. She took pride in taking care of the details, while never losing sight of the big picture.

Outside was a small and slightly sad paved area, surrounded by a high brick wall, most of which was taken up by bins. On top of the nearest, a small huddled shape could just be made out through a Tesco carrier bag. Cornetto pointed at it. "There lies your victim, clever cat. Take all the time you need, I'm sure you can get out over the wall when you're finished."

Buscemi frowned at the man's abrupt shift in tone, and swished her tail as he retreated back inside his cafe and closed the door behind him with a heavy click. Perhaps he had some customers to patronise.

Still, it was for the best. Buscemi had learned that humans who seemed to be otherwise perfectly comfortable with her uncommon intelligence and perspicacity tended to get a little on edge when she displayed much in the way of dexterity, even when she knocked on the balcony door to get the staff to let her in.

"Opposable thumbs aren't everything, losers," she muttered, popping out her claws, and slicing open the bag neatly.

The plastic parted like a ripe peach, to reveal Flollops. The unfortunate squirrel lay on his back with his paws folded across his chest and his bushy tail tucked between them, like a tomb depicting an ancient Crusader clasping his sword, chiselled in ageless rock.

The body was still fresh, and Buscemi almost expected him to squeak in protest when she batted him over to inspect his back.

"No wounds," she said. "And his fur's not singed, so it's not like he widdled over the wrong wire in that chiller or anything."

"You're short-staffed, yer southern Jessie. Where's yer comedy medical examiner eating a sandwich?"

Buscemi glanced up to see Stanley glowering at her down the length of his epic beak from his perch on the wall. "I'm investigating," she said with a frosty stare of her own.

The heron flapped down to join her on top of the bin. "Aye, I can see you're finally pulling yer paw out. About bleeding time, I might add."

"What killed Flollops?"

Stanley went quiet for a moment, staring intently at the tiny corpse. "I've got a few thoughts about that," he said. "But why don't we ask him?"

Buscemi flounced her tail. "If you're not going to be helpful, why don't you just go back to brooding under the bridge?"

Stanley gave an amused little squawk. "You watch close, little cat. Happen you'll like this bit."

With that, he reached out one enormous webbed foot, and planted it gently on Flollops's head. After a moment a faint nimbus of blue light began to glow around the squirrel's body. Buscemi took a step back, then pretended she needed to wash her ears, in case Stanley thought she was nervous or something.

"Deathless Guardians observe, and protect, but you don't dedicate centuries to preserving the sanctity of the city's bridges without picking up a few tricks along the way," he mumbled.

The blue light began to pulse more brightly, but Stanley looked troubled. "This ain't right," he said. "He should be back by now."

Buscemi scoffed, in spite of the light show. "Back to life?"

"Not exactly."

Stanley lowered his foot, and the glow faded away. "Your squirrel wasn't just murdered, little cat. His soul was taken... eaten. That's why he won't talk to us. There's something very wrong going on here."

***

Later in the churchyard, the Inedibles were doing their best to put together a more coherent report for their benefactor and boss.

"Garlic!" squeaked a hedgehog whose spines had become positively threadbare.

Buscemi waved her tail in slight confusion, and exchanged a glance with an equally bemused 'Ard Ren. "Bless you?" she tried.

"Nah, Greg's right," said Sean. "There's been bits and pieces of stuff going missing, from all the places along here. And it's all been stuff with garlic in it."

The fluffy hamster looked to his Inedible comrades for support. "We deducted that," he concluded, doing his best to look clever.

"Very enterprising," 'Ard Ren drawled, "and how did you culinary whizzbeasts *deduct* it was all 'stuff with garlic in it'?"

That provoked a chorus of excited chirps and squeaks, as the Inedibles went through a long list of the shops and restaurants that had been robbed.

"*Spoonful* it was just garlic!"

"*Pizza Bar* was garlic purée!"

"*San Remo* was garlic granules!"

"And *Tesco Express* was all that *and* the posh jars of curry paste," Greg finished with a jaunty snuffle of his hedgehog nose.

Buscemi arched her back and lay down, her own nose inches away from the hedgehog. "Michael. Against all our nutritional advice, your idea of a meal is still chunks of stale bread soaked in rancid milk. How would *you* know whether there's garlic in Tesco's curry paste?"

If the hedgehog felt in any way slighted by Buscemi's sceptical tone, he didn't dare show it. Instead he swelled with pride. "Easy. They dumped all the jars behind my compost heap, in Barn Elms Allotments. I read the labels."

It was 'Ard Ren's turn to frown. "*Why?*"

"I have a lot of time on my hands, OK? They dumped all of it there. It's a new compost heap of stuff with garlic, and it's bigger every single morning! They hit *Spoonful* last night."

"I know that, actually," Buscemi cut in quickly. "I learned it in the course of my *official enquiries*."

She paused for a moment while the assembled Inedibles made suitably impressed noises at her new status as an official crime-solving cat.

"Still," she mused, "*China Express* and *Spice of Night* must be furious. They put garlic in absolutely everything, don't they?"

"*China Express*'s chef was on the phone to his mum last night vowing eternal vengeance on the cursed souls who dishonoured their ancestors with this outrage," Sean agreed.

"Don't worry, he says that about everything," observed 'Ard Ren with a dry swish of her tail. "He's not even Chinese. His name's Giles and everyone else finds his nonsense quite offensive."

Michael nodded cheerily. "Fair enough. But *Spice of Night* hasn't been hit at all."

"Which means they must have did it!" Buscemi said, excited. "Done it. Whatever. And probably Flollops and that human interrupted them when they were robbing *Bohemia*, so they done the murder too. Did the murder. Oh, work out the grammar yourselves. I'm a genius. There! I solved my first crime! Who do I eat? They're kind of on the big side."

"*Or*," 'Ard Ren chipped in, "it just means they've not been robbed *yet*. You said it yourself, they put garlic in everything. They're the motherlode. They must be *next*."

"Meanwhile," said Sean, "what's to be done with the huge heap of garlic stuff mouldering behind Michael's compost heap?"

Buscemi stretched her paws as she stood up. "I don't know. Set fire to it, I don't care. I can't think of a single possible reason why some shadowy nocturnal force would want to systematically rid an area of garlic, and I certainly don't see any scenario where a large quantity of garlic might help protect us from this mysterious thief."

"Fair enough," said Michael, "especially as I suppose you'll be catching them and solving this crime tonight."

'Ard Ren gave a wise nod. "They'll surely strike again tonight. Detective Daintypaws, this could be your very first stake-out."

Buscemi shook her head indulgently. "I hardly think so, you daft fox. *Spice of Night* does curry, not steak."

She noticed the mice looking among each other a little uncertainly, as 'Ard Ren tapped a claw gently against her teeth. Buscemi thought a bit, and deflated briefly, before putting on her very brightest tone of voice.

"Oh. Yes, I see. So anyway, that's decided. Tonight I'll do my very first curry-out."

4 CURRY OUT

It was considerably later, and 'Ard Ren and Buscemi sat in Trinity Church Passage, the narrow lane that ran between the back gates of the parade of shops, and the back gardens of Merthyr Terrace and Trinity Church Road. They sat in the shadows cast by the garages, beneath a sign reading *No Ball Games*.

The brave little cat and the laconic sleek fox strained their respective ears as they heard the last of the *Spice of Night* kitchen staff locking up for the night.

"The manager gets the 33 bus out the front," 'Ard Ren whispered. "So we'll be OK for a few minutes, then I'll slip around the front just in case the thief tries to get in that way."

"Ah." Buscemi's ears drooped slightly. "I rather thought you'd stay here with me. And explain, not to put too fine a point on it, precisely what is expected of one in a curry-out?"

'Ard Ren was probably the one creature Buscemi knew to whom she'd make such an admission. They'd known each other a long time, and she knew the fox was far too refined to gloat at her ignorance. She was also the only creature in Barnes that could kick her furry bottom, which

48

tended to bring out her more deferential side.

"There's really nothing to it. On a stake - ah, curry-out, you just sit and watch the place until the baddies arrive, and then you Apprehend them in the Act."

"So I'm just going to sit here and stare at this back door?"

The fox hesitated. "Uh, yes."

To the fox's mild surprise, Buscemi purred and swished her tail in satisfaction. "Well, why didn't you say so? That's literally my favourite thing to do! You run along and stare at the front door. I've got this."

'Ard Ren swished her own bushy tail, and darted down the passage towards Holy Trinity Church. As she got to the end, she turned back for a moment. "Good hunting, little cat," she said, before disappearing to the right towards Castelnau, a single flick of the white tip of her tail gleaming down the passage like an indicator light.

"Yes yes, good good, fine," muttered Buscemi, and settled down for a really sustained bout of staring at the door.

She was almost disappointed that in the end she didn't have long to wait. After a mere forty minutes or so, she noticed it growing much more chilly, as her pretty fur fluffed up to keep her warm.

At the Merthyr Terrace end of the passage, she blinked as she realised the shadows were moving. Patches of darkness sliding over the walls and ground in spite of the orange glow of street lights.

That was peculiar, she thought. Possibly even remarkable, if she was the sort of cat to wander around being surprised by things.

The shadows were flowing in her direction down Trinity Church Passage, rolling and racing each other like raindrops down a window, accompanied by a distinctly ominous hiss as they slid over the concrete and bricks. Buscemi started to wonder whether she'd been entirely sensible.

Then, barely five metres away from the garages, the shadows pooled together in a huge mound of darkness. And then although nothing seemed to have changed, a human was standing in the middle of a patch of shadow. Buscemi relaxed. Her intensely acute eyes had been playing tricks on her, that was all. Staring into the darkness like that was always going to make her jumpy. She thought she'd seen darker shadows within the night, but really it had just been this man.

He *was* a man, wasn't he? He looked like one. He was about their height, with slick dark hair greying at the temples, and dressed in an elegant dark suit. Buscemi approved of humans wearing black. She took it as an indirect compliment on her own glossy fur.

Yes, nothing about this was strange. It was just a man with great taste and style, sneaking to the back door of the restaurant in the middle of the night, just in time for her to Apprehend him in the Act.

The dapper gentleman in the dark suit looked up and down the narrow lane and nodded in apparent satisfaction, before reaching out to the *Spice of Night*'s kitchen door. Buscemi's pointy ears flattened themselves against her skull as an icy gust of wind blew down the narrow alley. She blinked to avoid getting grit and cigarette ends in her dazzling emerald green eyes.

When she opened her eyes again, the strange man had gone, and a thick cloud of mist hung in the air. She bit back her primal urge to *hiss* as she saw the green-tinged cloud begin to stream into the door's keyhole.

In no time at all, the thick cloud had whooshed away into the building, leaving just a few stray wreaths of vapour drifting across the alley.

She couldn't follow. Even if the door wasn't firmly shut against her, she sensed those last threads of mist were somehow watchful, and would alert the being to her presence if she got too close.

That was fine, she realised. Her agile mind had been

jumping ahead even while her paws dithered. She had a sudden inkling as to what might happen next. With an excited swish of her tail, she darted back towards the bins behind the florist, even going out of her way to kick over an empty lager can, so she'd be mistaken for a clumsy drunk wandering home.

Swiftly she climbed back up to the flat roofs and trotted towards her own balcony, padding along silently on her dainty velvet paws. She slunk under the grubby white fence, and curled up under the round garden table, nestling among the plastic pots and bags of compost that heralded blonde staff's latest attempt to grow her own sunflowers.

Ensconced to her satisfaction, she again settled down to wait, her eyes fixed on the huge vent, which led up from the restaurant kitchens.

Sure enough, after just a few minutes the vent coughed up its usual gust of cumin-scented warm air, as the huge fan blades began to turn.

Buscemi was about to praise her own cleverness, when a muffled sound threw her into a panic. Puddles was dimly visible through the balcony door, scrabbling at the double-glazed glass, and no doubt whining at the top of his stupid squeaky puppy voice.

The fans were now whirring at top speed, and Buscemi was frantic. She didn't give two dead mice what Puddles witnessed of her nocturnal escapades, but whenever he whined like that, he had a tendency to bring the staff running before he could hose down the immediate area with his signature finishing move. The staff couldn't know about her crime-solving adventures. She couldn't quite articulate why, she just knew on an instinctive level that it would be a *bad* idea. They'd probably blog about it or something, knowing them, and then her potential for undercover work would be blown forever.

Sure enough, a light flicked on within the flat. They were moving about already, just when she was on the point of cracking this case!

Puddles looked back into the flat for a moment, as though he'd heard them coming, then resumed his scrabbling and whining as the fan whirred.

Then a spectral shape shot straight between the whirling fan blades and leapt into the air over the balcony. A giant bat, that seemed to glow with a deeper blackness against the night sky itself. And then she saw that it was carrying something in its viciously pointed talons; a small white shape almost a quarter of its size.

Buscemi knew she'd get no better chance to take down her suspect, but as she coiled to spring, it turned in the air to look down on her, and flashed vicious fangs in an open and gleeful challenge. It had probably been aware of her the whole time, confident in its ability to escape or defend itself. *Bother*, she thought, aware that she was never one to shirk a scrap, especially now that Puddles was watching. *Why do I care so much what this fuzzy little widdle-hydrant thinks, anyway?*

The bat flapped its wings once, and flexed its talons mockingly. *Here goes*, thought Buscemi, poised to leap...

Puddles suddenly turned, his ears drooping for a moment, then he bounded out of view, his tail wagging furiously. At the same moment the living room flooded with light, presumably the staff checking to see if Puddles had left any puddles... great, they were all going to watch her getting torn to shreds by a shapeshifting pensioner with a mouse fetish.

The light distracted the bat, however. It twisted away from the sudden blaze with a harsh screech, one wing sweeping forward over its face to shield it from the sudden luminance.

It was only a moment of hesitation, but it was enough. As the bat lowered its wing, dipping and lurching in the air, Buscemi smashed into it, paws first. Caught off-balance, the bat and the cat sailed clean over the balcony's fence and tumbled on to the flat roof beyond, eventually rolling to a halt on the skylight above *Spice of Night*'s kitchens. They landed in a jumbled tangle of paws, wings, and one *very* swishy tail.

The bat's eyes were flashing red with incandescent rage and it thrashed its wings so wildly that for a moment Buscemi was worried they were both about to take off. Then she planted a dainty paw on the winged rodent's chest, and extended her claws slightly until she was sure the creature could feel them digging in.

"You're *nicked*, sunshine," she growled, "unless you want a slash in that wing of yours so big you could shove your own furry little bum through it."

The flames dimmed in the bat's eyes, and its wings slumped in defeat.

Buscemi licked her nose and now wished someone *had* seen her being so brave and clever and daring. But she kept her voice as level and professional as she could. "That's better. Now give me one good reason why I shouldn't eat half of you right now and leave the rest by the door for the staff to step in tomorrow morning?"

There was a pause before the bat threw back its head and gave a long screech. After several seconds, Buscemi realised it was laughing. And several seconds after that, when she was just starting to get properly cross, she realised she was suddenly sitting on the dapper gentleman, her claws pricking the front of his blindingly white shirt.

The man was smiling, but the fangs didn't make that a particularly reassuring sight.

He spoke, in a surprisingly soft voice. "I would suggest you go ahead and try it now, but you're such a tenacious little imp that I'm not sure you wouldn't give it a damn good go."

Buscemi jumped from the man, her conflicting impulses regarding her crime-solving duties and strange humans battling to take priority.

Eventually she blinked at him sternly. "Hello. You can tickle my ears if you like," she told him. "But you're still under arrest."

The man sat up, raising an immaculately groomed eyebrow at the single muddy pawprint on his clean white shirt. He reached a hand towards Buscemi's adorably silky twitching ears, before shaking his head.

"Remarkable. You have a knack for compulsion that is rare outside the vampire race, little cat."

A ferociously tricky deduction clicked smoothly into place in Buscemi's agile brain. "You're a vampire? From Transylvania?"

The gentleman wagged an admonishing finger. "Please. That is quite a racist assumption to be making. And yet, yes. I am. Though I no longer prey on the blood of the living."

"I totally took down a vampire?" Buscemi did a delighted little caper before remembering that she was a grizzled crimefighter. The man's eyes flashed red for a moment and she sat back down on the cold, cracked skylight.

"If you've quite finished," the vampire said frostily, "I am indeed Dave the Impaler, whom some do call Saint-Germain, doomed to walk the earth for the rest of time, and a lover of -"

"Dave?"

Dave gave a slightly haughty sniff. "We immortals and children of the night must naturally change our names from time to time as the decades roll by, to escape the scrutiny of the ephemeral world. It turns out 'Vlad' doesn't provide much in the way of cryptic anagrams, even if you reverse it."

"Boring," sang Buscemi. "So why are you breaking into restaurants, Mr the Impaler?"

Dave rolled his eyes. "I thought you were cleverer than that. A vampire, stealing garlic from all the local shops and restaurants. Why would I be doing that, do you think?"

The little black cat's shrewd but lovely green eyes blazed with sudden understanding. "Vampires can't stand garlic! You were rendering the people of North Barnes defenceless, so you could – could..."

With a weary smile, the vampire gestured to a small white object that lay nestled in the nearby gutter. Buscemi's eyes narrowed as she identified it as both the object the vampire had been carrying from the fan when in his bat form, and as a plump head of garlic.

"... so that I could have a decent curry," he finished smoothly. "Tomorrow the chefs will come in to open their kitchen, only to find their cupboards empty of fresh garlic, dried garlic, garlic purée, and garlic and ginger paste. They will rush out, only to find the neighbouring shops are also out of stock. They will place orders for a fresh supply, of course, but in the meantime... that night they will prepare their dishes without the benighted allium, and I shall finally dine! Tomorrow at sunset, Dave the Impaler shall once again feast on his favourite, sacred, lamb bhuna."

Buscemi was aware that humans sometimes formed strange fixations, and she supposed there was no reason that wouldn't also apply to their unnaturally reanimated shape-shifting cadavers. And yet.

"That's a bit extreme, isn't it? Weeks of work, just for one meal?"

The vampire smirked. "You poor limited creature, this is a scheme brought to fruition by a master strategist. A single meal? I've already put in a huge delivery order, and I shall be gorging myself on chicken nawabi and keema naan breads for the next *fortnight!*"

The little black cat absently flicked a stray pebble between her paws. "Very nice. I suppose you must get used to over-planning, as the centuries pile up."

Thunder rumbled overhead as Dave the Impaler's eyes flashed red again. "I *like* curry. OK?"

"I think you and curry ought to get a room, but I find your story unconvincing. I'm in the middle of a jolly complex murder investigation, actually, and you started pinching garlic on the exact same day it kicked off. You're not telling me that's some sort of coincidence. Tell me what you know."

With a worried glance back at the balcony, which had long since fallen back into darkness, Dave fluttered his fingers and tried his best to obfuscate.

"Now now, let's just bear in mind that correlation doesn't necessarily confirm causation. If you hadn't been actively investigating, you might never have noticed my little peccadilloes. How do you *know* when I began putting my plan into action?"

"That's a fair point," Buscemi conceded, "and yet I'm not hearing an actual denial. You *do* know what's going on."

The vampire blew air from his cheeks in a vaguely despondent fashion before jumping to his feet and flashing a pointedly toothy grin. "I like you, little cat."

"That's Buscemi to you. Or Detective Daintypaws," she replied curtly.

"As I said. I like you, little cat." Dave strolled around the skylight, one hand behind his back as the other gesticulated wildly. "You know by now of course that dangerous forces are stirring in this suburb. That the world is a little more dangerous than it was last week?"

"Well, *duh*, frankly. There's murders in cafes and everything. *Last* week, all we had to worry about was whether the bin men would take all the cardboard boxes piled up outside the estate agent."

Dave waved his hand a little irritably. "Yes, yes, yes. Can the backchat, I'm trying to do you a favour here. *Something*, other than me, has returned to Barnes. Something immeasurably old. A plan decades in the making is entering its final stages. You're... close to the truth already. Closer than you realise..."

Another nervous glance towards the balcony. Buscemi mewed in frustration. "Is it past your bedtime or something? I did a very brave arrest on you, so blinking well tell me what's going on, that's how this bit works!"

Dave rolled his head around on his neck with a

revolting cracking noise, and shrugged. "I've told you all I can, perhaps all I dare. You're on the right path, and you're closer than you think to the answer. Do me a favour and get rid of that garlic, would you?" The vampire put his thumbs in his lapels, and continued. "There were two bodies in Bohemia that fateful morning, but one was nothing more than a red -"

"It wasn't, you know," Buscemi said, tilting her triangular head to a particularly wise angle. "It was a *grey* squirrel. The nearest reds to here are on the Isle of Wight, or Brownsea Island in Poole Harbour. Flollops was grey all the way."

Behind the flats, tyres screeched on Castelnau, the faint echoes bouncing across the rooftop plain. Dave shrugged again. "Very well. I can see you're... clearly an expert. Good luck, little cat. We'll speak again soon, of that I am sure. Don't forget the garlic. They're hardly likely to come up here looking for it, but I didn't sit through two jazz recitals and sixty quid's worth of cheese in *Bohemia* just to take stupid chances at the last hurdle.

With that, the vampire gave Buscemi a curt nod, strode to the gutter that ran along the rooftops next to Trinity Church Passage, and then stepped into blackness.

Alone by the skylight, Buscemi sauntered over to the plump bulb of garlic and picked it up in her jaws as though it were an errant kitten.

She padded back over to the balcony, deep in thought. "Why doesn't he just cook a garlic-free curry himself, if he's that bothered?" This was the mystery she pondered as she dropped the garlic in one of Blonde Staff's plant pots under the table, and did her derisory best to hide it with a few desultory paw scrapes of soil over the bulky shape.

The balcony door loomed, double-glazed and apparently impregnable. She'd been shut out for the night. Buscemi gave a long-suffering sigh, and began to curl up to sleep under one of the deckchairs.

A blood-curdling shriek split the night and she sprang

to her paws, her hair on end. Lights flicked on across the flats and all the way down Merthyr Terrace, and a few windows clattered open, bleary and confused human voices mumbling into the crisp night air.

They didn't recognise the noise at first, but Buscemi did. It was the cry of a fox.

'Ard Ren. Probably still waiting at the front of the restaurant.

In a flash, Buscemi sailed over the balcony fence. She turned in mid-air, landing on a skylight with a squeak as she skidded to face Merthyr Terrace. She lowered her pretty black nose to the ground and streaked along the flat roofs faster than even she thought she could run.

It was the quickest way to the front of the building, but also the hardest. There was no easy route down to the pavement.

But that was the Universe's problem. Buscemi sped up as she leaped over the final gutter, dainty paws outstretched as she flew in a graceful arc.

A small car was engaged in a slow parallel parking manoeuvre next by the kerb, and she bounced from its roof with the softest patter of claws, and landed smoothly on the tarmac.

Without bothering to check whether the driver had seen her, she surged on to Castelnau, skidding around the corner by the estate agent and hurtling past the derelict cocktail bar until she reached *Spice of Night*.

She ran past the huddled shape in the restaurant doorway at first, and had almost reached *Spoonful* when her agile mind caught up with her lightning paws and told her what she'd just seen.

"Oh," Buscemi said, stopping dead in her tracks. "Oh no. 'Ard Ren."

She walked back slowly, her tail swishing from side to side, and her teeth bared.

Sure enough, Ren was lying in the doorway, somehow tiny in death, her sharp eyes staring into the night in an accusing glare that was already turning glassy.

A low growl sounded in Buscemi's throat as she looked at her old...

"I don't have friends," she hissed to herself. "I don't have friends. But you just made a big mistake, whoever you are. *No one* makes Detective Buscemi Daintypaws Twinklefur owe them a favour. It gets right on my fur. And now I owe 'Ard Ren the biggest favour of all. I'm coming for you, and I *will* avenge her."

She hissed as the door up to the flats opened behind her, spilling warm light over the cold street and the cooling body of 'Ard Ren.

"... you were right, it was a fox. It's dead, must have been hit by a car."

Scruffy Staff was staring down at the small body, and Blonde Staff's lip wobbled as she joined him. "Poor thing," she said quietly.

Buscemi was about to say something cutting, but their sorrow for a creature they didn't know saved her the bother of feeling it herself. So she darted around their feet and up the stairs back to the flat.

She dashed into the living room and threw herself on to the window sill. She closed her eyes, but all she could see was 'Ard Ren's accusing glare.

"I don't have friends," she said fiercely. "Not any – I *don't* have friends."

5 LIBRARIES GAVE US POWER

"Yip! Yip!" Puddles was doing his best to disturb Buscemi's meditation, as she sat in the snug gap between the desk and the radiator in the spare room. She gave him a little hiss, but it was particularly thoughtful, and her heart wasn't really in it.

The daft little creature paused in his incessant whining, however, his tongue lolling out so he could switch to excited panting.

Oh, prickly hedgehog bums to it all, she thought best in front of an audience, even if the audience in question *was* just a leaky bucket of wee with a wet nose.

She swished her tail, importantly. "So. This is nothing more than a reminder to pursue multiple lines of enquiry, just to avoid the trail going cold in the event of a setback like this. I'm a victim of my own limited resources, that's all. But what have I learned from the garlic thefts and Dave the Impaler? That strange and powerful forces are abroad in this suburb, and that these forces appear to be common knowledge to those in the previously highly implausible supernatural community. So what do I do to investigate further? Dress up as a zombie cat (by not cleaning my fur for a full two hours) and start staking out the Holy Trinity Church graveyard to spend endless evenings dodging stoned teenagers in the hope of infiltrating a coven or something?"

"Hinn..." whined Puddles, causing Buscemi's back to arch in irritation.

"What an interesting observation," Buscemi hissed, determined to ignore the stupid dog's faux pas. "Of course, I need faster results than that, so there's only one course of action open to me. Only one place where I can find unglued morons who think they're clued into the nature of the cosmos. I'm going to have to go on the internet. If only my paws had an opposable thumb. I think I'll want to hold my nose."

"Yip!" Puddles agreed. He had a point. The staff spent a lot of time online, but their daft little phones were too small and fiddly for even her terribly dainty paws to use easily.

Which meant, she thought with a sinking feeling, that she was going to need to call in a favour.

It wasn't that she was particularly opposed to calling in favours, she mused, it was just that she'd never actually done anything altruistic enough for anyone to owe her a favour in the first place. She briefly wondered whether she could speak to Cornetto, but that probably wasn't going to make her look very good, asking for such basic help on her first major case and all that.

Buscemi gave a dainty little sneeze, which always weirdly seemed to terrify Puddles. The daft dog ran yelping from the room, and Buscemi clambered nimbly up to the window and slunk through the narrow gap.

It was a chilly morning, and Buscemi gave an adorable little shiver as she thought about her limited options. Fine, she'd have to fall back on her usual tactic; find someone gullible-looking, and tell them they could tickle her ears in exchange for her doing them the honour of allowing them to help her. Or... yes, there was a place she'd heard about. It would be their duty to help her, after all.

She jumped from the narrow windowsill to the top of the fan that had been the site of so much drama the previous night.

Pity it was broad daylight, she reflected ruefully. Dave the Impaler could have been a sure thing for helping her out, after she disposed of his stolen garlic. But in spite of the overcast sky, it would be many hours before that creature of the night could once more venture forth, and even then he'd be too busy stuffing his pale fanged face with keema naans and pints of Cobra.

As Buscemi trotted out on to Castelnau, she paused, then twitched her whiskers in satisfaction. The school run. Perfect. Cars ground along the road in an angry column of Chelsea tractors. On both sides of the road, suited parents dragged dawdling children, and pushed rattling buggies so fast that they were taking the corners on two wheels. Occasional parents on scooters weaved through the pedestrians, gaggles of school uniformed children trailing in their wake, blissfully unaware of the extent to which everyone else on the street loathed them.

It was bedlam. But while the scene presented a more dangerous prospect for a little black cat with legendarily dainty paws, it would also make her a lot more inconspicuous. She could go to the library, the one place she knew she could find help, and mingle with the crowds.

It took her maybe ten seconds to spot her mark. A little girl, brown pigtails, raincoat on a mild day, earnestly quinoa-stuffed packed lunch poking from the designer backpack that sat neatly across both her shoulders. She was stamping along the pavement, trailing her mother who was inevitably glued to her phone.

As the young girl walked past the junction between Castelnau and Trinity Church Road, Buscemi swallowed her pride as she rolled on to her back and held up her paws at the most adorable angle possible.

Sure enough, the girl's pronounced sulk evaporated and she beamed with delight before sidling over to the side of the pavement to rub Buscemi's tummy, with only the most cursory glance at her mother's retreating back.

"Mind the nipples, kid! Buy me a damn drink first!" Buscemi gritted her pearly-white teeth under the pre-teen onslaught, but sure enough in less than five seconds a shrill and slightly harried voice called out.

"Cheetarah, leave that poor cat alone, we're going to be late, darling!"

"She wanted cuddles, mummy," the improbably-named poppet protested in her cut-glass accent, but she stood up and scurried off to catch up anyway.

Job done. Buscemi rolled to her feet in a smooth movement, and her vivid green eyes radiated quiet satisfaction as she trotted along behind the girl. Toddler tailgating never failed. A cat wandering along a main road in broad daylight was unusual. A cat following a brat who'd stroked it was heartwarming, and never questioned.

As they continued along Castelnau, however, past the Tesco Express, and neared the bend at The Spinney, Buscemi began to wonder how long even an especially appealing cat like her could trail a kid before it began to look weird. As they passed the bus stop for The Spinney, almost exactly halfway to the library, Cheetarah turned. She started as she saw Buscemi still ambling along behind her, and she began to frown.

As her mouth opened to say something to her mother, Buscemi cut her off. "Eyes ahead and keep walking, kid. Or I'll personally shred your Hogwarts letter."

The little girl's eyes widened and she whirled to face forward. She started marching with a fresh spring in her step, and Buscemi briefly wondered whether she should feel bad about misleading the poor gullible child. She decided against it.

The small procession finally reached the junction with Washington Road, and Buscemi darted into a wide gravel driveway as mother and daughter continued down the long straight road that led to the High Street, a shadowy realm that Buscemi only really knew well thanks to the bi-annual trips to the vet that the staff persisted in foisting on her.

She was relieved to be rid of Cheetarah and the prospect of another mauling from her heavy hands, but Buscemi stuck close to the gatepost and lurked in the laurel bushes that screened the house from passing traffic. She slunk deeper into the bushes, doing her utmost to keep out of sight of the mansion's large bay windows, even to the point of ignoring all the delicious-sounding rustling noises from mice and small birds in the undergrowth around her. She was so far out of her territory that if another cat found her here, she wouldn't stand a chance of claiming she'd strayed over the boundaries accidentally. She'd have to fight. She might even have to... apologise.

"My genius ideas strike again," she muttered as she watched the twin queues of cars grind along the street in opposite directions. She was maybe thirty feet from her destination over the road, but it might as well be a yawning chasm.

There was a pedestrian crossing for – she hissed – humans, but she couldn't stand meekly waiting to cross the road at the traffic lights in broad daylight. She was already on the brink of becoming a sidebar story in *Metro* just for following Cheetarah for half a mile! But equally she couldn't just make a break for it across the twin lanes of slow-moving traffic. She'd seen too many fellow crime-solving cats succumb to the wheels of a dick white van driver, or even a militant cyclist.

"Curiosity might well have killed the cat," she reflected with a sigh, "but impetuosity would have been more apposite, if only it scanned a bit better."

Long uncomfortable minutes passed, and the flow of cars showed no sign of abating. If only there was some way of getting a message over the road to the one who ruled the library. Not that she needed any help or anything, but this looked like taking ages, and she had a heavy quota of snoozing to fit in.

Buscemi was beginning to feel despondent and in dire need of killing a few rodents to cheer herself up. Fortunately for the wildlife that surrounded her in the laurels, one of the heavy vans that was grinding down the road abruptly swung into the driveway, sending up a crunchy spray of gravel.

Ocado. Was there anything they couldn't do? As the van crunched to a halt, and doors opened and closed with vigorous clunks, and heavy footsteps swished through the gravel, Buscemi examined her options. When the driver finished their delivery, they'd have to pull back out on to Castelnau, which would mean, as long as they were turning right, there would be a brief moment when the road would be clear. It gave her a window to bolt across the street in comparative safety. Not ideal, but probably the best she could reasonably hope for.

"Hello? Mr Driver?" a cut-glass female voice rang out from the mansion.

The crunching footsteps stopped abruptly. "Yes, boss?"

"Would you mind *awfully* turning your van round so the doors face the house? My husband may have bought some Waitrose Essentials Cypriot Halloumi by mistake, and I'd simply hate any of the neighbours to see it and think one was strapped for cash, you see?"

There was a slightly perplexed pause, during which Buscemi surmised that the driver didn't often deliver to Barnes addresses.

He gamely tried logic. "I can't turn round on this driveway, not enough room. I'd need to back out on the road and do a three point turn in rush hour traffic. I'd block the whole street completely."

"Yes. Would you mind *awfully*?"

There was then a genteel crash as the front door closed. Buscemi could hear the driver muttering in disbelief as he climbed back into his cab, and even though it was all extremely convenient for her, she couldn't honestly blame him.

The van growled into life as it began to reverse back out of the driveway, exhaust spluttering and sirens beeping until every small creature or bird in the laurel bushes had either gone to ground or fled in terror.

As the van finished pulling out, to the accompaniment of a cacophony of furious car horns, and moved in a wide arc across Castelnau so it could back up into the driveway, Buscemi knew it was time.

She bolted from the bushes and over the pavement, narrowly avoiding tangling herself around the legs of the inevitable dawdling pedestrian who was bumbling along on the other other side. Ignoring their shocked squeal, she darted straight into the road, speeding along in the shadow of the Ocado van as it straightened up across two lanes of traffic.

The second half of the road was riskier than the first. The traffic was slowing rather than stopping completely, and then there was the bus lane; home to four different bus routes, cyclists, taxis, and anyone else who felt they were too important to sit in a queue on the normal road. Still, she was in the middle of the road now, so she was kind of committed.

Bleep! Bleep! Bleep! As Buscemi reached the bus lane, she heard the traffic lights from the nearby pedestrian crossing and purred with delight. That meant all the traffic would stop, apart from the cyclists whose smugness made them just *better* than other road users.

Sure enough, she scrabbled up on the far pavement only for her tail to be ruffled by the breeze of a passing racing bike whose expensive fibreglass frame was threatening to buckle under the bulk of its somewhat corpulent rider.

Buscemi's eyes narrowed as she watched the bike wobble away. If she saw it again, she'd pop a claw in its back tyre. But even the prospect of this summary justice was then swept away by a swell of euphoria. She'd made it!

Walked a whole half mile *and* crossed Castelnau. Her tail swished about her proudly as she realised that she was, indeed, a good cat.

As she sauntered along the pavement outside St Osmund's Church, and turned into the small garden area in front of the library, however, her elation ebbed away.

The library was closed. The double doors were shut, and she could see no lights within the boxy building.

"Oh, fiddle-dee-ree," said Buscemi, but even the heaviest locked door is no match for a pretty little cat, especially one with her cunning and resourcefulness.

So she sat in front of the main door's largest glass panel, and pawed at it softly, while mewing softly, her eyes saucer-wide.

And then she waited.

After a while, the fur between her pointy ears began to rise and tingle. She looked around, and dropped into a defensive crouch as she spotted a plump black and white cat that was lying on the recycling bins and watching her with quiet amusement.

"Oh, don't mind me," the stranger yowled in plummy tones. "I'm interested to see how long you intend to keep up that performance, given the library won't be opening for another three quarters of an hour."

Buscemi did her best to relax. This was the very person, after all, whom she had been counting on meeting.

"Henry the Library Cat, I presume," she purred.

The black and white cat yawned. "And you... my mind *may* be wandering, but I deduce, you're Buscemi the crime-solving cat? And they call me Dewey now, because I'm a complex system fulfilling a simple function. It's a librarian's joke, you know. Quiet and packed with references. Whereas Harry was starting to sound a bit too uncouth and UKIP for Barnes."

Buscemi twitched her whiskers. "If we're being pedantic, Dewey, they call me Detective Daintypaws. I have a badge and everything."

She shook her head until the bottle top on her collar started to jingle like a bell against the buckle. Dewey gave an involuntary little hiss, and her heart swelled with pride at his palpable envy.

"Anyway I'm glad I caught you because I thought I'd let you Assist in my Enquiries," she continued with her most gracious air.

Her magnanimity was brushed off with a derisive swish of Dewey's tail. "I don't know. I'm incredibly busy and important."

Buscemi nodded. She was on Dewey's territory, and standing on his draughty concrete steps. He was fully entitled to be stroppy about it, even if she did suspect that it came rather naturally to him. "I thought you probably would be, but my colleague did *particularly* want me to try."

Dewey was opening his mouth to say something suitably cutting, when there was a loud thump from behind the recycling bins. After a couple of slightly quieter thumps, a webbed orange foot appeared from behind the bottle bank, followed by the end of a long pointed beak and, eventually, by Stanley.

"Bugger me gently, you were only bloody right, little cat!" The heron strutted towards Buscemi, his neat plume skewiff and his wise old eyes blazing with excitement. Then he caught sight of Dewey, and abruptly reverted to his one-legged fishing vigil pose of stately elegance. "Who's this big southern Jessie?"

Buscemi licked her nose, savouring every delicious nuance of the moment. "Hello Stanley, deathless guardian of Hammersmith Bridge. Mr Dewey, a cat who sleeps on the library carpet while small children sing nursery rhymes, was just explaining why he couldn't assist our terribly pressing murder enquiry."

"Was he now?" Stanley put no particular inflection on his question, but he tilted his sleek head just enough that the sun glinted from the water droplets that still clung to the sharp end of his long beak.

Dewey fawned, though not without throwing several hate-filled glances at Buscemi. "There was no disrespect intended, Guardian. Had I known this cat was somehow engaged on Council business, I would never have..."

"Oh aye. Would you 'eck as like. Harken unto me, my Order watches over this world without reward, complaint, or exception. For we understand the nature of the forces that threaten your very plane of existence, and we don't care how many snooty moggies we have to eat in order to discharge our sacred duty. Are we in understanding on this, like?"

Buscemi tried not to purr too loudly as she watched Dewey's fur bristle in helpless frustration. Finally the cat licked his nose, and batted idly at a dry leaf in a display of studied nonchalance. "Let it be noted that I gladly extend the Council every possible aid," he said finally.

"Great," said Buscemi, so eager to get down to work that she decided to ignore the pointed emphasis in the library cat's voice. "So, let's get on the line and web the surf for clues!"

Dewey opened his mouth at that, but Stanley chose that moment to tilt his head, and his very long spike of a beak, to the other side, so he settled for rising to his paws with a haughty swish of his plump tail, and turning his back on them.

"If you would just wait here, I will need a moment to open the, ah, tradescat's entrance." And with that, Dewey slunk away around the corner of the building.

Stanley didn't make a great deal of effort to wait until the cat was out of earshot, before whistling in disbelief. "What a daft ponce! Did you spear his stickleback out the ornamental pond or something?"

Not for the first time, Buscemi wished she had eyebrows to raise, she just knew she'd be brilliant at it. "Something," she agreed, eventually. "It's a cat thing. Like if another heron came bothering your bridge vigil."

"Pfft," Stanley snorted. "Try and get rid of young

Derek over from Barnes Bridge, this past fortnight. All these blethering questions. 'Can we do this? What happens if that?' But we're deathless guardians, after all. It's probably different for you furjobs."

"Probably," Buscemi said with a gracious *mew*, licking her paw and running it over her velvety ears, unconsciously. "You just have to keep an eye on bridges and prevent the collapse of civilisation and that. *I* have to worry about who's eating shrews on my territory behind my back, so it's pretty vital stuff, I can tell you."

A 485 bus thundered past in the strained silence as Stanley tried to process that, but then he shook his magnificent plumed head. "Aye. I expect. But you were right. We were watching the weeds along the bank, just like you said, even though Drake and I thought you were plain barmy, to tell you the honest truth. And there was only a blinking *vampire* wandering along the path before dawn this morning, bold as you like, sniffing the grass ever few yards!"

A strange sensation settled over Buscemi's shoulders, and she realised with disgust that it was perilously close to guilt. She should have told Stanley sooner. "Ah yes, that would be Dave the Impaler, leaving nothing to chance, and checking the banks for wild garlic. Classic obsessive vampire behaviour. I arrested him last night, but I'm forced to admit he has a watertight alibi for the murder."

"Alibi?" Stanley spluttered. "He's a blinking vampire! Wandering around Barnes as bold as brass? This is a code red, little cat."

It was Buscemi's turn to snort. "Hardly. He talked big, but I took him down single-handed on the rooftops. Which was simultaneously no big deal but also kind of bad-ass, if you must know. If you'd like to put me forward for a medal or something, I probably wouldn't object."

The heron blinked rapidly a few times. "You, a little black cat with a smart mouth, *arrested* a vampire?"

"Oh I didn't need to *really* arrest him in the end. He

doesn't know anything, not even what colour squirrels ought to be, so I Eliminated him from my Enquiries." Buscemi purred a little in spite of herself, proud to be using proper crime-solving terminology. "That's why I'm here, to Pursue Other Lines of Enquiry. Because I'm being dogged and methodical, you see."

There was a brief pause as Stanley tried visibly to collect his thoughts. "It's a vampire," he said finally, sure of that at least. "A vampire that turned up at the exact same time as your bodies. Vampires aren't exactly commonplace, even south of the river. There must be a connection. They're always plausible and charming, but they're vicious harbingers of carnage."

Buscemi snickered softly at the thought of how clever she was about to be. "This one isn't. He's more of a harbinger of *korma*. He just wants a garlic-free curry, and then he'll be on his way. That's why he was down by the river. Checking for wild garlic, in case the chefs got it into their heads to go foraging."

"Keep watching the weeds," Stanley said in a whining impersonation of her voice that Buscemi decided she'd overlook just this once. "You *knew* there was a vampire involved and you still gave us that cryptic little excuse for a hint? Drake and I could have had our throats torn out! Those pallid ponces don't prat about!"

"Not a vampire as such. I just observed that local businesses were having their garlic pinched with a systematic rigour that suggested an obsessive personality behind the incidents. What? A mysterious intruder is obsessively spiriting away SW13's supply of garlic under cover of darkness and I'm *automatically* supposed to assume it's a vampire?"

There was a dry hairball-laced cough behind them. The investigator and the guardian turned to see Dewey standing in the library's open doorway. "I threatened to shred picture books until the staff opened the door for me. But I was reluctant to interrupt such a fascinating conversation about grocery stocks and the local flora."

Stanley glowered again at the aloof library cat, but with the door open at his back and on his own territory, Dewey barely flinched.

"Aye," said Stanley. "We need to talk more on this, little cat."

"I'll come down to the bridge at sunset," Buscemi replied, importantly. "I've a feeling we're going to crack this whole case tonight."

With a single and slightly disdainful thrash of his enormous wings, Stanley leapt straight in the air from a standing start, his head tucking into his chest as his long neck concertinaed into a graceful s-shape. He was gone in the next instant.

"Shall we?" Dewey asked, tossing a disdainful glance at the spot where Stanley had been standing."

Buscemi followed Dewey through the doors with a heavy heart, bracing herself for even more territorial nonsense, exacerbated by the fact she couldn't retaliate, as her business here was too urgent to allow the situation to escalate.

As soon as they crossed the threshold, however, everything changed. The two cats were faced with a vast open space with walls lined with bookshelves and computer terminals, and a central reception area from which clusters of free-standing shelves radiated like spokes. An abrupt transformation came over the prissy cat.

"An *actual* Guardian all the way down here, that's bonkers," he said, purring with delight. "And I'm going to be Assisting with Enquiries? Really?"

Dewey's chest was swelling with pride so quickly that his paws were in danger of floating away from the scuffed old doormat across which they were trotting.

"You've changed your tune," Buscemi observed, with a dry sideways glance at the librarian.

"Oh we have to observe the form *outside*, I don't want any old local moggies barging their way into this sweet deal

I've got going here. Sorry if I came on a bit strong, I can be a bit of an ogre," Dewey trilled.

Buscemi let that apology hang in the air for a moment while she savoured it.

"Anyway," she said eventually. "I'm investigating the mysterious murder of Flollops Chez Arbre in *Bohemia* earlier this week. I'm pursuing multiple lines of enquiry, but I need to consult the Internet, and look into any other strange local happenings."

"Oh, you don't need the internet here, we have The Papers!" Dewey seemed very sure of himself, but that was also Buscemi's speciality, so she took it with a pinch of salt.

She hesitated as he swaggered away towards a low rack on which hung five or six limp bundles of white paper, and one pink. "And they'll tell me about strange goings on in Barnes?"

Dewey's eyes misted over, and he rolled reverentially on the ground in front of The Papers. "Oh yes. They know *everything* that happens, right across the entire world."

In spite of herself, Buscemi was impressed. "What, even *Putney*?" she breathed.

"From Putney all the way West to *Chiswick*," Dewey assured her, and indicated the nearest bundle. "Consult this one, for example. The *Mirror*. It reflects all society back at us. With pictures and everything."

"Jezza Fury At Tory U-Turn," Buscemi read, and gave Dewey a stern look.

"The *Mirror*'s messages must be interpreted," Dewey said in a lofty tone of voice. "For example, this must surely refer to the traffic jam outside a few minutes ago, when an Ocado lorry pulled a three point turn on Castelnau, and clagged up three lanes of traffic."

Buscemi was so impressed she almost forgot to be aloof. "That's amazing, how can it be so up to date?"

"They're replenished each morning. It's the first argument between my staff here, every day." Dewey yowled over his shoulder as he pulled the *Mirror* from the rack until it slithered to the floor like a damp towel knocked from a radiator, its pages spreading across the thin carpet in a slow motion avalanche of newsprint.

He continued, mimicking squeaky human speech with cruel precision. "They're like 'have you brought in the papers?' 'Of course I did, they were right on the step, duh!' 'Well, no one's put them out.' 'Oh, I thought you wanted that cup of tea *before* lunchtime.' They get *ever* so worked up about it, I can only assume it's some kind of ritual. But the texts follow broad patterns over the weeks, especially about immigration."

"Immigration?" Buscemi asked.

Dewey's nose twitched. "Yeah… As magic scrolls go, they're all mostly kind of racist."

He stepped away from the newspaper spread over the floor. "The important thing here is to…"

Before the exuberant cat could stop her, Buscemi pounced on the paper with all four paws, her exciting claws flexing deep into its pages. "Right, magic *Mirror*. Tell me what you know about the *Bohemia* incident. Did 'Jezza' do that too?"

She paused, peering at the text and images that thronged around her forepaws. "How does this work? Which bit do I look at?"

After a moment's thought, Dewey peered at a back page headline just under Buscemi's charming nose. "It says here: 'Messi dominates the Kop'?"

Buscemi purred. "That's just it! It was all so very messy that the cops had no idea where to start! What else?"

"Ah…" Dewey frantically scanned the pages of newsprint pinned to the floor by the purring detective's dainty paws. "How about 'DJ brushes off sex claims?'"

"No *way*," Buscemi mewed. "There were *six* garlic thefts, and now this Dee Jay is trying to deny they ever happened? He must be working with Dave. Dewey, I had my doubts, but I think we're close to some serious answers, here."

"There should be something, we just need to keep looking. Mind you, this is Barnes, there's really not a lot going on. They've resurfaced the church car park next door, and the staff got a new doorstop."

Buscemi pulled down *The Guardian* from the the rack, perhaps that might hold some clue that Stanley could decipher. "A doorstop? They keep a door *open*? How do you get by without a door to stare at until they open and close it every five minutes?"

Dewey sniffed with a trace of his former haughty demeanour. Buscemi realised he was covering up an instinctive nervous reaction, and paused in her kneading of *The Guardian*'s front page to watch the cat with interest.

"I found another door to stare at," Dewey said, eventually. "That thing gives me the creeps. I call it 'Abyss'. Because like Nietzsche (Modern Western Philosophy: Germany & Austria - 193) says, every time I stare at it, it just stares straight back into me. Creepy owls, always hated them. Who looks at a pigeon and then gives it the power to kill?"

Buscemi shivered. "My staff got one too. Stole it from outside a charity shop, in a bag full of bugs."

"Yeah, mine found theirs in the skip when they resurfaced the car park. And it's the fire exit they leave it propping open, so of *course* I get the blame for every half-dead mouse that limps in to die in the back office. As if I have time to go hunting when there's so much to do in here."

The cats looked around at the deserted library. "I suppose it's much busier when the humans come in," said Buscemi kindly. "Staff, eh? Who'd have 'em?"

Buscemi was maintaining the banter, but she was aware of a stray thought at the back of her mind, calling and waving for attention. She dismissed it; after all, she didn't interrupt her crime-solving just because her staff were standing on the roof terrace and shouting for her, so she was jiggered if she'd be bossed around in the privacy of her own head.

Both looked round in alarm as a voice rang out across the empty library. "Did you put the Papers out?"

The staff's voice sounded exactly like Dewey's earlier impersonation of him, she had to hand it to the book-finding cat.

The question prompted a lengthy burst of trivial human argument which floated over the shelves towards them. Buscemi frantically scanned the ocean of jumbled and increasingly creased images and text that surrounded her dainty paws. The answer must be here somewhere. Or maybe this idea had been even more of a dead end than last night's curry-out in Trinity Church Passage.

"There must be *something*. Help me out, Dewey!" she hissed, then blinked. Dewey had vanished.

At that moment a heavy trainer-clad foot stomped into view around the nearest set of shelves.

"Oh bother," said Buscemi. She froze, her adorably pointed ears flattening against her head.

A bearded human stared down at her, his face flushing red and screwing up in surprise and rage.

"Eileen!" he squealed, "there's a bloody *cat* shredding today's Papers!"

The other voice called back, indignant. "I only just opened the back door! Don't tell me it's been in here all night? Get rid of it! Chuck it outside!"

Buscemi looked into the man's furious face, and recoiled from the malice she saw glinting in his deep-set eyes. "Over-reaction, much?"

"With pleasure," the man snarled, flexing his fingers as he reached out for the little cat.

Buscemi saw the tell tale coating of orange dust on the man's fingers, up to the second knuckle. The bounder had clearly been stuffing his face with Cheesy Wotsits for breakfast; she was glad Castelnau Library did not, to the best of her knowledge, possess a Shakespeare First Folio.

And he wouldn't be getting his sticky fingers on her, either.

She hissed at him. "You may try. But you can not *chuck*, that which you can not *catch*."

With that, Buscemi exploded into movement. Letting out one mocking 'miaow', she darted between the man's trainers, and out into the centre of the library.

'Eileen' was sitting behind the huge central desk, looking important at the keyboard of a computer. She scowled as she saw Buscemi dash into view, with several pages of The Papers still clinging to her paws.

"Accursed vermine-consorting sycophantic feline," the librarian growled in an unnaturally deep voice, her eyes flashing an all-thing-considered quite unexpected shade of crimson. "We will flay your soul for this outrage!"

"Yeah?" Buscemi said, *pushing* her words so even the stupidest human couldn't help but hear, "well, kiss my fluffy yet sleek tail, you pallid book-sniffing leech!"

Feeling the thud of trainers behind her, Buscemi easily dodged another grab from Beardy's be-Wotsited digits and charged straight for the central desk.

As she'd expected, Eileen's unexpected spot of red-eye hadn't improved her reactions beyond those of standard staff. When the daring black cat leapt up on the desk, bounced into Eileen's dark hair, and then launched herself towards the back of the library, her only comeback was a guttural snarl.

Behind her, the man crashed into the desk just as Buscemi began to sail through the air, tattered scraps of the travel supplements fluttering down from her paws like glossy snowflakes.

The librarians' lips slammed together, and, after the shock of that initial impact, they began to kiss deeply as the flurry of shredded package holiday adverts fell about them. The man reached up to stroke Eileen's cheek.

Meanwhile, Buscemi hit the ground running, several metres on the far side of the desk, and she surged away towards the back wall, one single photo of Theresa May still clinging to her right hind paw as she dragged it across the carpet.

Through the wooden door on the rear wall, she could hear the dreadful off-key wailing of a primary school music lesson.

Behind her, Eileen smelled the Wotsit dust on the man's hand that was touching her face, and she hurled him away with disgust, and a distinctly guttural growl.

Buscemi shuddered at the mere thought of the cavalcade of infant squeals that would accompany any attempt to bolt through the primary school. Instead she veered right, towards the computers that lined the library's back wall. She'd known all along they were her true objective.

Four ageing desktop computers were ranged along the right hand side of the library, making for a stab at what the kitten of detectives was pretty sure the librarians would have persisted in calling a 'multi-media hub' until far too recently to be even slightly cool.

One of the computers' rickety blue-cushioned swivel chairs was already occupied; a middle-aged man in an anorak who was squinting intently at the chessboard that glowed on his screen, while coughing so aggressively that he sounded as though he was trying to start a fight in a pharmacy queue.

But Buscemi's eye was drawn to the monitor next to Garry Coughsparov. Some sort of local blog, apparently. "Council Probe As Planning Office Approve Riverside Property Basement Extension" ran the headline, but that was boring. Instead, she was more interested in the accompanying photo, of a crowd of Barnes residents who seemed to be celebrating outside a huge house. One of them was caught frozen in the act of pouring what appeared to be champagne into tall glasses that were brandished by several others, though the bottle's label was carefully tilted away from the camera.

The Barnes resident holding the bottle was none other than Scruffy Staff. He was pouring cheap fizz into Blonde Staff's glass, with their glittery friend, and Cornetto, and… was that Eileen the growling librarian completing the bourgeois tableau as they waved their own flutes in the background? Other locals made up the numbers, indistinguishable cookie cutter dark-haired lawyers, and fair-haired brand managers.

Buscemi ignored the story. The story didn't matter. The staff had been sloping off for the odd few hours in the evenings for weeks, and Puddles was clearly tiny enough that he didn't really need the exercise. The answer had been right in front of her all along.

Dewey materialised beside her, with not a whisker out of place. He licked his paw thoughtfully as he followed Buscemi's gaze.

"Oh, *that* - she's so angry she wasn't at the front of the photo, you know. The Wotsit lad asked why she was so bothered about some C-List celeb's cellar conversion, and she tried to slam his head in the automatic doors."

Buscemi frowned. "That seems… excessive."

"Maybe. These *literary* types, you know." Dewey stretched to let out a particularly satisfying yawn. "She's in some sort of secret club though. She can't stop banging on about it. They meet underground and practice close harmony singing or something. In the men's toilets, apparently, which the other one found *hilarious*, for some reason. Until she punched him."

"Interfering animal *filth*!" A demonic cry rang out right behind them.

"Ah yes, I don't think your Eileen likes me," Buscemi said.

A nearby bookcase crashed to the ground, to reveal the librarian, red-faced, red-eyed, and her hair on end.

"I'd better leave, I think I found what I needed. Thank you for your hospitality, Dewey. I hope your staff calm down soon."

Dewey gave a slightly prissy sniff, and wandered off towards the children's books, as Eileen lunged towards Buscemi.

Buscemi was tired of running, especially as it was a long walk back to her flat as it was. She dodged Eileen's grasping hands, and raked her wrist with her claws. "Overdue."

The librarian screamed in pain, shock, and rage, but she stopped to clutch her wounded hand, and Buscemi strolled away.

She headed back towards the small wooden door that led to the library's back office, ducking round a bookcase as quickly as she could so that Eileen couldn't see which way she was going.

Then the man stepped out in front of her, looking almost as enraged as his grabby colleague.

With a sigh at all this palaver, Buscemi put her head down and charged again. She darted through the back office, past dusty old PCs and piles of books that were presumably waiting to go out on the shelves, past a little sink with a kettle and a box of teabags, and finally saw the fire exit ahead of her, just as Dewey said, a glimpse of an alleyway, some dustbins and a wooden fence beyond it.

The sight of the grey plastic owl propped against the heavy door brought Buscemi skidding to a halt. She shivered in spite of herself as its glassy orange eyes stared into her with an accusing glower that was frozen in time.

She shook herself as lumbering footsteps shook the floor beneath her. This was no time to get freaked out by ornaments. To show the world that she was the bravest cat they'd ever seen, Buscemi ran straight for the doorstop, jumping on its loose head and launching herself into the fresh air of the alleyway where she landed on top of a dustbin with a clatter.

"It's gone outside!" she heard the man's voice call back into the library, and she breathed a sigh of relief. Finally she could stop running about the place like some sort of excitable puppy.

From her vantage point perched on top of a broad black rubber dustbin lid, Buscemi looked down at the open door. And shrank back as she met the owl's gaze a second time. It was staring up at the bins levelly. How was that possible?

She remembered Blonde Staff's owl had a moving head, she supposed she must have moved it accidentally when she bounced off it.

Yeah, that must be it.

Buscemi hopped lightly down from the bin and wandered down the alley towards Madrid Road. She could walk straight up the quieter residential street and be home in plenty of time for a quick nap before she kept her appointment with Stanley. She'd send one of the Inedibles down to let him know she'd found some suspects at last.

And then she could think about the smug little owl smile that was plastered across the doorstop's beak.

6 ESCAPE TO DANGER

Buscemi stretched and opened her eyes. She narrowed them against the low evening sun that was pooling on the cushion where she lay. Damn this comfortable sofa. She'd only meant to close her eyes for a quick five hour nap, and now it was nearly time to go and meet Stanley and Drake.

She hopped down to the floor, and trotted towards the balcony, grimacing with every step as the tips of her splendid claws pitter-pattered against the wooden floor like rain on a greenhouse roof. Ordinarily, Buscemi was rightly proud of her long sharp claws, but they were impractical for the stealthy work ahead of her tonight.

Still, easily fixed.

With a graceful flick of her tail, Buscemi turned and dashed over to the owl doorstop, her paws sounding like a nest of mice eating a bag of crisps.

As she popped out her claws and looked at them with a mix of admiration and regret, she spoke softly to the owl.

"I hate to do this to a fellow predator, but you are pretty pointless."

With that, she stood on her hind legs, dug her front paws into the thing's plastic wing, and raked them downwards.

It was a pretty good scratching post, she had to admit. She could feel her claws being worn down with each scrape, but only a few faint hairline grooves in the doorstop gave any indication of the use Buscemi had found for it.

Shredding the thing with abandon, Buscemi began to purr. She'd be back to her deadly silent best in no time, thanks to this thing!

The front door slammed, and Buscemi leapt back to the sofa, where did her best to look nonchalant.

"Hruff! Huuuhhrrr... uff!" The scruffy one had brought Puddles back from his walk then. Buscemi was starting to wonder what the point was of taking the stupid creature out so often if they *weren't* trying to lose it.

"Buscemi Daintypaws," the staff yelled in his most irritating sing-song voice, "I've got a present for you!"

She'd barely had time to butt her head against the cat flap of her mind palace before she realised this was a flimsy attempt at subterfuge, and the present was either flea treatment, or the threatened collar. Scruffy Staff hated fiddling with the noddy syringes, so would be more inclined to pretend to forget about flea treatment until the more dextrous Blonde Staff arrived home. That already made it more likely to be the collar, which rose to a 95% probability once you accepted the existence of flea collars to cover both options at once.

Fight/flight? *Flight. Now.*

Before she could uncurl from her studied nonchalance, however, there was a strangled cry from the living room doorway.

"What have you *done*? Come here, you stupid... moggy!"

Buscemi tried to protest. "Woah! This is the 21st Century, you do *not* use the m-word. That's *our* word! *Our Word*."

Her protests were silenced by Scruffy Staff's hand gripping her firmly by the scruff, and dragging her into the hallway. "Stop that noise," he said brusquely, "you *bad* cat."

"What's twisting your melon, man?" Buscemi twisted her head as best she could in the psychologically-paralysing nerve pinch of Scruffy Staff's unbreakable scruff hold.

As he swept her towards the landing with his jaw and two of his chins set, she clocked the pointless owl. Her claw-sharpening gashes still looked like barely hairline scratches to her, but by the tacky thing's taloned feet, grey plastic shavings lay in a pile of curls like the ribbons on Elton John's Christmas presents.

"Seriously?" she yowled. "All this drama over a scratch on a doorstop? I once did a wee on your duvet three nights running until you had to sleep under a *curtain* and you were more together than this."

Scruffy Staff swore as he wrenched the bedroom door open with his free hand, flinging Buscemi into the room while trying with his foot to block bloody Puddles from bounding in after her.

The pile of clothes she landed on was actually pretty comfy, but for the look of the thing, Buscemi came up hissing. Too late.

"You stay in here while we clear up the mess, and get your collar ready." He actually slammed the door in her adorable face, leaving her with a last glimpse of the puppy staring at her with an expression you could only call, well, hangdog.

Imprisoned, Buscemi swiped a fly out of the air in frustration. She had to get to the rendezvous, she couldn't rely on her rag-tag posse.

What was going on here? The staff were predictable, compliant. It was the whole point of allowing them to accommodate her, in spite of that wretched dog. If they were going to start getting weird about her defacing their kitschy stolen ornaments, she might as well take her chances with the mad cat lady who lived over the post office opposite.

Lost in her thoughts, she didn't know how much time

had passed before she heard the scratching at the bedroom door, and the soft keening.

"Forget it, Puddles. There's nothing in here you've not chewed, even if I *would* open the door."

"Hinn! Hinnnnn!"

Buscemi rolled her vivid green eyes. "You're really not an asset to my investigation, you know."

She was about to turn her tail and curl up on the bed in a suitably aloof fashion, when she saw something pale slip under the door. A curved, flat, grey object.

Almost like a heron feather.

The cat's alert gaze leapt to the window, where Stanley and Drake stood on the ledge outside, silhouetted against the rapidly darkening sky, and rapping their bills fruitlessly and silently against the double-glazed pane.

She scrambled up to the windowsill, using a pile of Blonde Staff's university paperwork as a stepladder. The window was shut, but not locked. She looked at the two levers that secured it, and gave one of them an experimental tap with her paw. It budged a little. She could do this, but she'd have to hope the staff just assumed they'd left the window open by mistake, or even the scruffy one might finally think to start wondering about her capabilities.

She heard a heavy footstep in the hallway, far too heavy to be Puddles again, and she put both her dainty forepaws under the handle on the left. With all her feline strength, she heaved against the handle, and was shaking with the effort as it finally lifted far enough to open the catch.

Stanley and Drake fluttered their wings in celebration, but panting Buscemi turned to the second handle.

Her first push revealed the second handle was stiffer, and it barely budged. But she *had* to do this. Her case was breaking!

Just an inch in front of her pretty nose, Stanley and Drake froze in horror. Buscemi followed their eyes, and mewed softly under her breath as the bedroom doorknob began to turn.

She was too late, she was going to be fitted with a bell that would take her whole *days* to break, and she'd be next to useless on this investigation.

She strained one last time at the window, felt the handle shift by a grudging degree or two as though just to mock her defeat.

"Yip! Yip! Yip!" Puddles let out a series of shrill barks from the hallway. Buscemi started, but the knob stopped turning.

"Don't be a silly puppy," Scruffy Staff was muttering. Buscemi shook her head, but when she turned back to the window, she saw the handle was finally high enough for her to open the second catch.

She pushed the heavy window with all her might, pressing against the glass with both forepaws and her furry forehead. It moved slowly at first, centimetre by agonising centimetre. A chilly draught blew straight through the gap and ruffled the fur on her tummy like a soon-to-be-clawed small child.

The door knob rattled again. Puddles was still barking his heart out, but it seemed Scruffy Staff was not to be distracted again.

Buscemi yowled into the worried faces of Stanley and Drake, just inches away from her through the glass.

Then Drake tucked a wing under the slowly rising edge of the window, and with a sudden rush Buscemi was falling through into the cold night air and landing heavily on the guttering.

A wordless groan of dismay from the flat behind her suggested that Scruffy Staff had seen her go, but Buscemi and her two friends scrambled up to press themselves against the wall directly beneath the windowsill.

"Bushy, come back!" the portly idiot wailed into the night, poking his head and shoulders through the window and looking left and right in panicked desperation. "Who left the window open? Ah, probably me, better not say anything…"

"Hinn…" whined Puddles, jumping up on the sill next to the staff.

"Get down, puppy-duppy, we can't lose you out there. Buscemi knows the way back."

There was more barking and squeaking, and the window thumped shut.

Buscemi let out a deep miaow of relief, but the two birds were looking at her in concern.

"What?" she demanded.

"What the hell was all that about, furjob?" Drake asked.

"God knows, I just sharpened my claws on his tatty plastic owl, and he went mental."

Stanley stretched his neck to its full height in order to peer through the window. He blinked. "That pup's putting up a right scrap to keep that plonker busy. It's a good job we found him."

"All right," retorted Buscemi. "I was biding my time to make a dramatic escape, *actually*. Did you talk to him?"

"In a manner of speaking," said Stanley thoughtfully. "We gave him the feather and told him to find you, but he just wagged his tail, yipped a lot, and widdled on the floor. Is he simple?"

Buscemi sighed. "The simplest. He only came to find me because when people give him anything he feels he has to show it off to someone."

Drake flapped his wings, drawing both their attention. "Right. Now we busted you out of there, where are we off to?"

Buscemi's mouth dropped open as Stanley and Drake looked at her expectantly. "Well…"

"Hinnn…" Even Puddles was gawping at her now, through the window, those absurdly huge shaggy paws resting on the sill, and his tail flapping behind him. Oh, great. Again she felt strangely panicked at the thought of failing in front of this stupid little puppy.

"Well, we're looking for a place full of people, by the river. But… different people. Coming and going. Underground. In the gents toilets, would you believe? And a glamour cast over it all, so no one gets suspicious."

Stanley shook his head with grim finality. "Nay. There's no magic cast on my river as I don't know about. No glamours hereabouts."

"Nah, blood. But is like it *has* to be magic?" Drake was looking uncharacteristically thoughtful. "A glamour's just a magical nudge, innit? Dulls what people actually see, makes things feel better than they actually are."

"A bit like…" Stanley squawked, then coughed. "No, you say it, lad. It's a good thought, I'll not steal your thunder."

"It's a pub, innit?" said Drake, with a grateful quack in the heron's direction. "The calming effect of the booze stops 'em from seeing anything strange going on, and if they do see someone carrying on, they just assume they're pissed."

Stanley and Drake spread their wings. "So, the White Hart it is," Stanley said, and turned towards the edge of the roof.

"Hold on," said Buscemi, "I'm a resourceful, clever, and very charming little black cat, and I often surprise myself with my ingenuity so it kills me to admit this but… I can't fly."

"Talk a lot, don't you?" said Stanley, turning back from the gutter with an amused glance at Drake. "Can you not just scurry along behind us? It's only a couple of miles at most."

"I most certainly *can't.*" Buscemi was appalled, and her dainty paws throbbed at the mere thought. "For one thing, I'd have to cross some of the world's busiest roads, and for another…"

A smooth voice broke in from above. "… And for another, time is of the essence."

Dave the Impaler was standing on the roof, two floors

up, a black cloak swirling around an immaculate dinner jacket. He was looking down on the road, and on the three intrepid crime solvers.

His lips barely moved, but his words carried down to them as clearly as though he was standing right next to them. "You have uncovered… a portion of the truth" he said with a smile, and it was unclear whether it was the sight of his bared fangs or just his condescending tone that had Stanley's plume bristling almost perpendicular from his head with rage.

"Yes, a portion," Dave continued, nodding. "Enough to put you on your guard, and to take you to your final test. But for that, I believe I might be of assistance. A small cat is no burden to one such as I."

"We're fine, thank thee very much," snarled Stanley through a gritted beak, and even Drake looked shocked at his tart tone of voice. "So sling yer bleedin' hook. The cat can walk."

"Forgive me, but I rather doubt that," Dave replied.

He stepped out into empty air, and floated gently down towards the gutter. He carried on talking as he descended.

"I'm not unaware of your status, Stanley de Montfort, nor of the reactionary views your Council harbours with regard to my kind. Ah! We could wage a most glorious war up and down this suburb and, make no mistake, part of me would relish that. But we have other enemies, older foes, and I believe you begin to suspect what you are about to face."

"That's as maybe," Stanley blustered, as the vampire's brogues alighted on the guttering between them., "but what's all this nonsense about time running out?"

"It is. In three important respects," Dave declared, pointing a bone-white dramatic finger down at the street. Scruffy Staff was scurrying across the road, a bulky shape tucked under his arm. As Buscemi watched him reach the turning into Lonsdale Road, she saw several other pedestrians scuttling in the same direction, each carrying a similar burden. Some were wrapped in brown paper, while others bulged from a Waitrose Bag For Life. But all of them were unmistakably large plastic owl sculptures.

"They're on the move, Guardian. That's the first point. Second, the waiters in the restaurant below are starting to wonder about all the strange noises coming from their awning."

Drake regarded the vampire with a sceptical eye. "Your hearing's that sharp?"

Dave cocked an eyebrow and treated the mallard to a thin smile. "Oh, you'd be amazed what you can pick up without the auditory background radiation of fresh blood pulsing in your ears. But on this occasion, no. They were commenting openly on the noise a few minutes ago when I was still in the restaurant. Which brings me on to the third point…"

Dave the Impaler reached inside his dark cloak, and withdrew a small white plastic bag containing several bulky rectangular shapes. "My Lamb Bhuna will be getting cold, and as our furry friend here will tell you, I have gone to quite some lengths in order to acquire it."

Buscemi let the f-word go as she hadn't taken her eyes off the junction of Lonsdale Road, where Scruffy Staff had long vanished from sight. "The owls. They're magic. The staff thought I'd been hunting, but it was the owl, feeding off prey, sucking the life out of them. The owl's framed me and I nearly had to wear a bell. They're going down. Let's do this."

Scruffy Staff was an idiot, and would be first against the claw when the feline revolution came. But until that glorious day, she had to admit, he knew which variety of Go-Cat to buy. He got out of bed to tend to her whims the moment he heard her shredding his paperwork through sheer boredom. She'd seen him standing at the back door bleating her name with increasing desperation for *hours* on cold nights when she'd been far too busy and important to come into the house. Collar or no collar, she felt she ought to save him from being brainwashed by a doorstop. She'd finally got him trained.

Ignoring Stanley's contemptuous glower, she wound herself around the feet of Dave the Impaler. After several seconds, he finally tutted quietly, and scooped her up with the hand that wasn't full of takeaway curry.

Once she was within the circle of Dave the Impaler's cloak, the endless rumble of Castelnau's traffic and Heathrow's flightpath was muted to the faintest murmur. "Don't be nibbling at my poppadoms," said the vampire in a low voice, before leaping into the air, Buscemi cradled snugly in the crook of his arm.

With Stanley and Drake right behind him, the four crime fighters dipped low over the pavement, narrowly avoiding a 33 bus as they pulled up in the thermals that rose from the road's traffic-warmed tarmac. The negative g-force tugged at Buscemi's suddenly weightless body as they soared towards the windows of the Bright Horizons nursery on the far side of the road, and Dave banked to the right.

As he followed the movement almost immediately with a sharp turn to the left as they took the corner on to Lonsdale Road, Buscemi anticipated and rolled with the slight movement of the vampire's shoulders. This flying business was brilliant! Surely she could manage it if she tried really hard? So far it just seemed like doing a really big jump.

As they straightened out around the corner on Lonsdale Road, just below the level of the rooftops, Buscemi dared to look down. The feeling of supremacy was intoxicating as she watched the distant asphalt flow far below her forepaws, while street lights wheeled past her head. She should always travel like this, she decided. Dave was a bit pretentious, but with careful training, he would probably make pretty decent staff.

"Don't even be thinking it," the vampire whispered in her twitching velvet ear.

Buscemi's eyes widened. "Can you read my mind?"

"I hardly need to, you're a cat. And we're flying too low for me to be wearing this shape."

As they passed the junction with Boileau Road, the vampire surged upwards, and Buscemi mewed as her stomach yawned again.

In a moment they were a clear twenty feet above the rooftops, and Buscemi began to feel distinctly chilly, despite her excitement and the vampire's warm cloak enveloping her.

She wasn't the only one feeling out of her comfort zone. To her right, Drake thrashed upwards to draw level, quacking hoarsely with emotion. "Jokes, man. What you doing, blood? This is - whack. Whack! Whack!"

Stanley wasn't any more impressed, but was at least a little more composed as reached their altitude. "All right, leech. Happen you bear in mind this isn't my first air raid? We're carrying a low-flyer and a ground-crawler. We're too high."

"Do as you like, goldfish gobbler," Dave replied in his most urbane voice, sounding a little bored. "In this form, I look like an overdressed estate agent. The mortal residents of Barnes endure enough estate agents without wanting to see them wheeling past their skylights, I assure you. I'll stay up here."

Both birds darted a worried glance at Buscemi, but they continued their high-altitude escort. After a moment, Dave gave a quiet nod of satisfaction before swooping to the right, just as the houses on that side of the road petered out to be replaced by the endless playing fields and darkened windows of St Paul's School.

"A few crimes for you to solve there, I wager," the vampire whispered. Buscemi purred, surprising herself, but maintained her prim, no-nonsense tone. "That would be inappropriate, Mr the Impaler. Investigations by the proper authorities are ongoing."

Away from the road, even Stanley seemed to relax.

"We're making good time. I suppose the cat couldn't have followed us cross country in any case."

Dave the Impaler gave a polite nod to acknowledge the Guardian. "We take a longer path, along your precious river. Those bearing the owls cannot be trusted, and the statues themselves have senses that you cannot guess at. Better to lose a few moments now and keep the element of surprise."

"I can't help noticing that I seem to be taking a back seat in my own investigation," said Buscemi, though she didn't feel as cross as she thought she ought to.

"We're just the… staff, little cat, think of us as larger Inedibles," said the vampire, and banked to the left, giving Buscemi a magnificent view of the river.

The meandering Thames coiled around her field of vision like a silver snake in the moonlight. The ancient river was lined by trees on the Barnes side, and a solid wall of expensive houses and the Fuller's brewery on the Chiswick side.

Buscemi's eyes drank in every detail hungrily. How small her own territory was, with all this world to explore!

They were flying faster now they were clear of the road, the wind whistling around Dave's cloak as they zipped over the trees and cast a faint flickering shadow over the river.

As Buscemi watched the shadow skipping over the river's gentle moonlit waves, her over-stimulated brain finally began to catch up with her delicate ears.

"How did you know about the Inedibles?" she asked quietly.

The vampire didn't have breath to catch or a pulse to quicken, but she sensed his nervous reaction immediately. "Who knows? Maybe I can read your mind," he said, with a dry laugh.

Troubling possibilities started to line up in Buscemi's thoughts. "I doubt that," she told him. "Or you'd have been a lot more careful about picking me up."

"Woah, blood, what's with the red-eye?" Drake called through the night air, and Buscemi realised the vampire's eyes were blazing with rage once again.

"Let us… discuss this… when we have reached our… destination," Dave hissed between clenched fangs.

"A destination I'm only reaching thanks to your intervention? Again, I rather doubt it."

The vampire began to shake in the air, and Buscemi was troubled to realise he was laughing at her.

"After all and what do you propose, little cat? Far above the deep waters as you are, what choice do you have but to trust me?"

Buscemi had lived long enough to know that her instincts weren't always correct, but that it was always safest to act on them.

"Stanley," she called. "Change of plan, make sure I don't get my tail wet."

With a really determined wriggle, she backed out of the vampire's arm around her tummy, and climbed up on to his back, under his cloak.

"Foolish creature!" Dave the Impaler hissed, as Buscemi scrambled her way up the vampire's back. He began to writhe and tilt from side to side, in an effort to shake her off.

Buscemi flexed her claws, gaining a firm purchase on his jacket. "I thought I was a rather clever cat. Did I perhaps get a bit too clever, Mr the Impaler?"

It took her a bit more wriggling with the cloak's heavy material, but in a matter of seconds she had climbed on top of the billowing garment, and run up to perch on the vampire's shoulder.

"Stop this!" roared the vampire, his eyes burning with ruby flames.

"I'm sorry, Dave. I'm afraid I can't do that. Now, take me down. Or suffer the consequences."

With great care in the buffeting wind, Buscemi unhooked one forepaw from the cloak, and pressed it gently to the vampire's neck.

"You presume to threaten me, *animal?*" The vampire snarled. "I walk in eternity. No mere *cat* can harm me."

"Even one who buried your garlic for you last night? With *this* paw?"

Dave froze. "That was many hours ago. No trace could possibly remain," he said very slowly and carefully.

Buscemi shrugged. "Yeah. You're probably right."

She swiped the vampire's neck hard with her dainty claw-studded paw, and was rewarded with a bloodcurdling scream.

Bright green slime bubbled from the tiny scratch, and their flight stalled. The vampire and Detective Daintypaws began to tumble from the sky, towards the churning river.

"Make your mind up, blood!" Drake quacked as he struggled to match their rapid descent.

"We're crashing, *Ducky*," Buscemi yowled.

The vampire seemed no more keen on splashing into the river than Buscemi was, and was angling his body towards the left bank as best he could, his free hand clamped to the bubbling wound in his neck.

Buscemi could see they weren't going to make it. She took a deep breath, and launched herself in a flying leap from the top of the vampire's head.

Corkscrewing through the air towards the river bank, she quickly realised that there was indeed a little more to this flight business than doing a really big jump.

"Sorry, Flollops. Sorry 'Ard Ren," she whispered as she plunged towards the hungry water.

Just a few feet from the waves, Stanley crashed into her falling body, and she clung to his strong long neck.

He couldn't bear her weight, but the heron managed to slow her descent, and they crashed to the shore together.

Seconds later, a blossom of spray erupted from the water, just a few yards away from the bank.

"So much for Dave the Impaler," Buscemi panted.

Stanley struggled to his feet, looking worried. "Nay,

little cat, it'll take more than a dunking and a dirty paw to off that bugger. We can't tarry here."

Drake crashed to the ground between them, shifting from foot to yellow webbed foot in an uncharacteristic state of agitation.

"No, blood, why here? Why here? *Not* cool…"

"What's tickling his whiskers?" Buscemi asked Stanley.

The heron was a little more composed, but also seemed nervous. He began scanning the trees that lined the towpath. "Ah, well. Happen you'll remember that spot of bother the other month? Zombies and the like running around, all sorts of fuss?"

"Yes, of course. I was a bit of a hero that day, as a matter of fact." Buscemi had slept through the whole thing.

Stanley eyed her for a moment, sceptical, before returning his attention to the towpath. "Right. Well. It wasn't just humans that turned, and they weren't all dealt with."

"What are you talking about, Stanley?" Buscemi demanded. She was cold, battered, and in no mood for messing about.

Hooonk! The stentorian cry echoed from the trees, as an indistinct shape reared up from the bank. Buscemi took an involuntary step backwards as the thing shambled into the moonlight. She took in its long but abnormally twisted neck, its ragged feathers, and its pitted black beak, encrusted with dried blood.

"Zombie geese," Drake said with a relish that Buscemi found quite uncalled for.

"Grains…" the goose honked again.

"Huh. That's pretty funny," said Stanley. "But we need to get out of here."

Buscemi began to trot towards the treeline. "If you say so. This walking roadkill's hardly going to stop us."

"Grains…" The goose began to drag itself after the little cat, but painfully slowly.

She didn't understand what all the fuss was about. Daft birds. At least Dave had been fast, and shape-shifting, and tricksy. This zombie thing was so useless she was already considering giving it a job with the Inedibles.

"Grains…" Buscemi froze. That fresh moan had sprung up from the trees ahead of her at the top of the bank.

"Grains…" A second zombie goose emerged from the shadows under the trees. And then a third, further up the towpath.

"Grains…" More and more of the shambling creatures lurched on to the river bank. The three adventurers were surrounded.

"Stan? Can you fly?" Drake asked, as they retreated slowly towards the shore, pursued slowly but inexorably by the undead waterfowl.

Stanley gave his wings an experimental flap. "Oh, aye. But -"

"But neither of you have any intention of abandoning Detective Daintypaws to a bunch of zombies. Right?" Buscemi cut in, with a sharp look at both of the birds.

"Right," they chorused, a little shamefaced.

They were going to have to fight their way through, and while Buscemi knew she'd have the edge in terms of speed, the geese had greater range with those long necks, and sharp black beaks.

This was awful, she thought as she backed closer and closer to the water's edge. She'd make a terrible zombie cat, she could see from their ragged feathers and dark stains on their legs that the pitiful monsters had no grooming schedule at all!

Drake and Stanley were hardly bothered by a bit of water, but they stopped at the water's edge anyway, flanking Buscemi. A semi-circle of a dozen or so zombie geese surrounded them, shambling closer, and closer, and then stopped just a few feet away.

Buscemi extended her claws, and arched her back in

readiness for the battle. Then frowned. "What are they waiting for?" she muttered out of the side of her mouth to Drake.

"Beats me, blood," the duck replied, earning them both a sharp look from Stanley.

Which was when the faint voice piped up behind them. "And you… beat me… but they will not come closer to one such as I. They smell my power… even now."

Dave the Impaler no longer looked like a crazed immortal demon or an ageless terror of the night. Washed up on the shore, his immaculate eveningwear reduced to waterlogged mush, and his thin dark hair plastered flat across his translucent scalp, he looked rather pitiful. Particularly with his clawed fingers pressed weakly against the crusty but bloodless gash in his neck.

"I underestimated you, little cat," he said with a plaintive look to Buscemi.

She bristled. "People are always saying that like it's a compliment! I'm Detective Daintypaws! I have a *badge*. If you're underestimating *me*, it's like you don't respect or believe in badges at all. *And* you don't even know the difference between a grey squirrel and a red fish!"

"You're… right, of course," Dave replied as soon as he was reasonably sure Buscemi was finished, and not just pausing for breath. "It is rare for a vampire to be bested, however. Perhaps you did not know this."

Buscemi waved an airy paw. "Oh, people keep saying that too, but I think it's just made you over-confident."

"Perhaps so. *Anyway*, you must believe I was never meaning you any harm. As I told you, ancient forces are stirring, and you are the only one who can prevail. All I wanted was to get you where you need to be, to deliver you to your destiny."

The vampire broke off, coughing up a torrent of foaming green slime. It was hard to tell whether he was still afflicted by the garlic, or by the several pints of Thames water he must have swallowed before washing up on the shore.

Buscemi took a delicate step backwards to avoid the nasty mess. "Well, you rather fudged that up, didn't you? You should just tell people things, instead of trying to be all mysterious. Now thanks to you, my trail's gone cold, my paws are slightly damp, and I'm going to have to wait for *minutes* for someone to pick me up and carry me home."

"Little cat, I'm *dying*," the vampire gasped.

"Yes, and my paws are slightly damp," retorted Buscemi. "But there's no point banging on about it, we just have to soldier on regardless, apparently."

The vampire's voice had become fainter than a gnat's bleat. "Please *listen*! I need some warm, fresh, b -"

Drake took a sharp waddle backwards, far too close to the ring of zombie geese that surrounded them. "You're not getting any fresh blood from me, uh, blood!"

"*Bhuna,*" finished the vampire in a thin whisper that still somehow managed to convey his exasperation. "Perhaps I should just die here, this conversation is as relentless as undeath."

"Aye," said Stanley, "maybe that'd be best. But... happen as I found your little doggy bag floating a few yards out and fished it out. Thought it was carp," he finished with a fierce glower that let all and sundry know he was still the Deathless Guardian of Hammersmith Bridge and wasn't about to start getting soft on vampires or owt of that sort.

Buscemi and Dave the Impaler immediately and simultaneously recognised the earthy but piquant aroma curling from the bulky bag that dangled from Stanley's formidable beak. The brave detective knew the scent of a balti curry from years of long evenings spent crouched under the restaurant's fan on the balcony. And if any doubts still lingered about the veracity of Dave's claims to be in town purely for garlic-free dinner, the frenzied greed on his face as he recognised the smell was enough to banish them forever.

His clawed fingers lashed out to tear the bag from the stately heron, and his eyes flashed red with one last burst of strength as he tore aside the white plastic to reveal a cardboard-topped foil takeaway container.

Under Stanley's withering glower, the ancient vampire hesitated or a moment, before lowering his bedraggled head over the container. A moment later, the crime solvers exchanged uneasy glances as a gurgling, sucking, slurping noise emanated from the vampire.

"Surrounded by slavering zombie geese?" Buscemi prompted after a while.

There was no movement from the tableau of takeaway carton and wet vampire, though Buscemi repressed a rare shudder as she watched his torn neck close up and heal, the nasty crusts that edged the wound fading away in the moonlight as she watched.

Stanley was straightening his neck in order to clear his throat importantly, when with an ecstatic gasp, Dave the Impaler threw back his head, then howled at the moon.

The vampire's mouth and chin were covered in orangey-red goo, which dripped from his bared fangs. "I live!" he hissed in triumph. "Truly I am Dave the Undying!"

Two jagged holes could be seen in the carton's lid, twin red-rimmed puncture marks in the lamb bhuna.

"Uh, zombie geese," Drake reminded him, as one of the creatures behind him let out a restless honk.

Dave tried to stand, but slumped to his knees in the mud. "Still weak," he hissed. "But these low undead will do my bidding, for all that. Fly, my vassals."

"Grains…" honked the goose directly behind Drake.

"Try harder, Snotferatu," Stanley spat.

"I am not quite myself," Dave admitted with an embarrassed sniff. He pointed at Buscemi, and his fingers had never looked more talon-like.

"My minions," he whispered, his voice now carrying far

over the river's choppy waters in spite of his low tones, "take this one to the sacred place. To the destiny she has yet to forge."

Buscemi yowled as downy feathers pushed at her insistently from behind. She could hear Stanley and Drake squawking in alarm as the zombies surrounded her.

"Worry not, little cat," came Dave's tired but increasingly confident voice. "Put your dainty paws on their webbed feet. They will complete your journey while I rest here, they will follow by instinct the lines of ancient power that swell through this place. They will take you, at last, to the end of all things."

The vampire's voice trailed away at the end, and Buscemi looked over to him, only to realise she was already ten feet in the air, slung low from the tattered feet of zombie geese flying in a strangely close formation.

She felt her fur rise instinctively as she saw water slipping by beneath her paws again, but then Drake and Stanley bobbed ino view just below her.

"You're safe, man, innit?" Drake quacked. "We don't know what that muttonsucker was banging on about, but Stan and I are right here."

Stanley didn't look at her, but shifted his long beak into a particularly determined position. "Aye, little cat. Rest a while till we get there.

"It's time to end this."

7 THE BATTLE OF THE WHITE HART

A duck, a heron, and a black cat had set off from Castelnau, but three comrades alighted in the deserted garden of the White Hart, or so Drake liked to think.

Buscemi sprang down from between the legs of the zombie geese, and as soon as she hit the ground, she gave a good hiss at the close-flying gaggle of undead poultry.

The birds didn't seem to react to her hostility, and the formation banked to the right to loop around and fly back up the river, without a pause.

Drake watched them go. "Stan, we need to up our game. Zombies, blood?"

The heron gave the duck a sharp look, but sighed. "Aye, lad. I've been a soft touch too long. But that ends tonight."

Buscemi ignored their Guardian talk, and looked over the garden. No sign of the Staff, or anything untoward, it was just a normal pub garden, studded with picnic tables that stretched towards some open patio doors that led into the bar. It was no use, she had to get inside. It was probably too much to expect Flollops's murderer to be standing around in the garden where she could get to them easily.

She called up to the heron, "We need to get inside, but these places only let blasted *dogs* in. We need some sort of diversion, so we can get inside."

"Don't worry, I'm a walking diversion." Stanley spread his wings and gave them a good shake before thrusting his head forward and marching stiff-legged through the gaping doors.

Silence fell for a moment, rolling out over the picnic tables before popping against the river as it lapped against the bottom of the garden.

"That's a damn heron!" a raucous voice called from within. The scrape of chairs and digital clatter of mobile phone camera shutters couldn't mask Stanley's triumphant cry.

"Herons live in the river, you know," trilled one nasal voice from inside the bar, "the tide must be coming in really high this evening."

Drake rolled his eyes. "Dese folk are jokes, man."

A fresh roll of gasps rolled from the empty doorway. Buscemi craned her neck. "He's hopped up on the bar and stuck his beak in a tall jar of peanuts," she said after a moment.

"That's probably the diversion," Drake said helpfully, then realised he was alone. By the time he'd finished speaking, Buscemi seemed to have become a blurred black arrow flying straight through the pub's french windows.

Vaguely aware of some quacking nonsense behind her, Buscemi darted into the pub. In her experience, the morons who ran these places were happy to leave out water for a dog of all things, but they tended to get all *unnecessary* when she showed up with a freshly-slain sparrow. Maybe you just weren't supposed to bring your own food?

The crowd was pretty sparse; coffin dodgers and a few students were dotted around the low tables and deceptively uncomfortable sofas. In any case, all eyes were on Stanley, who was now making a spirited attempt to tip back his long neck and wear the peanut jar as a heron space helmet.

"Rub, Buscebi!" Stanley yelled through the thick glass and a beak full of bar snacks. Mentally correcting his words, Buscemi put her head down, and ran even faster, streaking towards the staircase at the other end of the bar.

"Back!" With a thump of wings that spilled wine from two abandoned glasses on nearby tables, a second heron screeched like a velociraptor trying to go to the toilet through a fossilised bum. It thumped up into the air from behind an armchair in front of the fireplace, screaming and hissing into Buscemi's face.

Claws springing into the dense carpet to try and slow her charge, Buscemi darted a glance back towards the bar, as much to escape the newcomer's piercing mad gaze as anything. "Er, Stanley? Little help?"

With his own furious squawk, Stanley tossed his elegantly plumed head, sending the peanut jar hurtling towards the new threat.

The other heron twisted to avoid the missile, which crashed into the chimney breast and sent a blizzard of nuts pittering into the grate. The enraged bird took its eyes off Buscemi, and locked on to its assailant.

"Bloody hell!" Stanley exclaimed, leaping from the bar on to a table, as the last of the human drinkers ran for the door. "Derek? What are you doing here? Who's minding your bridge?"

The other bird screeched again, snapping its long beak several times. Buscemi could see the door leading to the staircase. It was several feet to the right of Derek, and with the enraged bird's attention fixed on Stanley, perhaps she could...

As soon as she took a first slinking step, Derek's head jerked back to her. His peripheral vision really was *very* good.

"I asked you a question, Derek! Who's minding your bridge?" Stanley's voice was clear and firm, and Derek slowly swung back to face his fellow guardian.

"This is Barnes Bridge business, Stan. Wind your neck in."

"Bridge business? Is it 'eck as like!"

"The owl-god rises – a new order for all of us. None shall be permitted to interfere with that, least of all the Deathless Guardians." Derek's calmly insistent voice was almost as disturbing as his former screeching. Buscemi licked her nose and looked between the two herons. Stanley was perched on the table, one foot planted squarely in a ploughman's lunch, while Derek shifted his weight from foot to foot. The Barnes Bridge guardian was a little bigger than Stanley, his plumes flicking from his head at an almost perpendicular angle. He looked a bit younger, but Buscemi had no idea what factors were important in a heron smackdown. She could settle most disputes with the right icy glower and warning growl these days, but when she'd been younger, fitter, and faster, she was ashamed to admit that she'd had her over-confident tail handed to her by no end of wiry old fleabitten moggies.

"Yer big southern jessie," Stanley snorted, breaking the moment as only he could. "*Owls?* You've thrown your lot in with a bunch of dry-crapping swivel-headed peanut-beaked moon botherers? You'll thank me for this leathering once I've knocked some sense into you."

Stanley spread his wings, jerked his head forward, and roared with murder in his voice. He leapt into the air, with a single wingbeat that flattened nearby stools, and reared back his plumed head.

Derek hesitated, but quickly regained his confidence, screeching back with equal savagery. He put one enormous foot forward, poised to leap.

There was a sudden crash as the heron's foot skidded on the pile of peanuts in the grate, and the bird went down in an unruly tangle of wings, spindly legs and elongated neck. No creature can get itself tangled quite like a heron, but there was no time to appreciate the spectacle. With a triumphant hiss, Stanley surged forward, closing the distance between the two birds in a flash, and clouted Derek's head with one powerful wing.

Unable to marshal his wayward limbs in time to dodge, Derek reeled from the blow. But as Stanley followed it up with a vicious jab to the throat from his long beak, the younger bird fended him off with a flailing kick from one long leg.

Battle was joined, and Buscemi was captivated. A cat fight would already be over by now, with Derek clearly put in his place. But these crazed birds were clearly tenacious and persistent, and Stanley's energy must surely be flagging after his long and arduous flight from Hammersmith Bridge.

Derek howled in pain and rage as Stanley got in a lucky peck, grazing his spiked beak hard down one of the younger heron's legs. Perhaps Stan was the favourite, after all.

As Derek put his head down for another charge, Buscemi jumped at the touch of a powerful wing on her left hind leg. Drake had crept up behind her. "How many distractions do you *need*, blood?"

The penny dropped as Stanley beat his wings in Derek's face, and flicked his eyes to the cat and the duck in the corner. When he let out his next terrifying screech, Buscemi was ready.

"OK, blood. On the count of – oh, you've gone." Drake's nasal quacking receded into the distance behind her as Buscemi streaked away towards the door.

She didn't hear anything to suggest the crazed heron had spotted her move, but she certainly wasn't daft enough to look over her shoulder and check. Instead, she hurtled through the door and threw herself down the spiral staircase she found behind it.

Tasteful pub paintings blurred past her piercing green eyes as she tumbled gracefully down the stairwell, sticking as close to the central pillar as possible, to minimise the distance she needed to cover.

She half-fell, half-ran and, in spirited defiance of the laws of fractions, half-flew down in a matter of moments, but her paws finally touched down on the basement carpet squarely and firmly.

It was another disappointment. Buscemi had only wandered into a handful of pubs over the years, and always in search of the kitchen or a warm spot in front of an open fire, but she certainly recognised a completely mundane corridor to the toilets when she saw one.

She dashed on, barely hesitating when she heard a powerful crashing noise shake the floor above. Stanley struck her as being about the only bird she wouldn't want to cross, and if it was getting a little frisky in the bar, she was pretty sure it wouldn't be Stanley breaking furniture with his face. He could handle some coked-up little underling, and even if he couldn't, well, it wasn't as though he'd want her trying to pitch in on his side. Typical bird: deep down he was an utter racist. Well, she wasn't in the mood to broaden his perspectives tonight; she'd just have to hope he won the day.

A second crash refocused her attention, as it came from the corridor ahead of her. A portly bald man was lurching from the male toilets, tucking his shirt into his already bulging trousers and apparently oblivious to the fact that the last part of his wee had been accomplished down the inside of his trouser leg.

Buscemi did her best not to punch the air. This incontinent waddling oaf wasn't just her ticket to the men's toilets, but the fact he was acting so normally was a sign, albeit a vulgar one, that there was currently nothing untoward and cultish going on in The White Hart's toilets at that exact moment.

"Kitty," the man slurred, and Buscemi bounced into motion again. With a few powerful bounds, she was in front of the erratic toilet sprayer, purring to confuse him.

"Hold the door a moment, or I'll ask you again using

people words, and you'll be so freaked out you'll never enjoy a pint of vodka again," Buscemi suggested. Sometimes the direct approach was the most effective.

Without another word, the drunk swayed to one side, his bulk propping the door open while Buscemi slipped between his legs. There wasn't much of a thigh gap there, but thankfully she just managed to avoid brushing against his 'accident'-stained trousers.

He was a big enough bloke that he'd left the door wide open, but Buscemi had got her lovely tail stuck in a french window back in 2007, and wasn't risking that again. She shot through into the inner sanctum of the gents' toilets, which she now knew to be the nerve centre of the whole terrible affair.

At the sight of an empty tiled room, festooned with urinals and electric hand driers, Buscemi stopped in her tracks, her honed claws scrabbling for purchase on the smooth tiles.

"Empty? But it can't be! Dewey was *emphatic*! Stupid bloody ragdoll!" Buscemi was seething as she paced between the toilet door and urinals, ignoring the baleful stare of austere sepia-tinted photos of Barnes Bridge back in the 1930s. Buscemi was focused on her case, but she still threw occasional quizzical looks at those wintry landscapes, to see whether she could make out the tell-tale plumes and beak of a heron caught in mid-stride on the dismally pebbled foreshore.

"It's this room, blood!" Drake crashed through the door and flopped to the floor with a quack and a heavy thud, prompting Buscemi to wonder whether he'd simply flown into it at full tilt.

"It's a dead end, for berks who wee on their own shoelaces," Buscemi spat, having wrinkled her nose at the results of her preliminary smell-based deductions.

"Smell harder, furjob," Drake hissed. "Even I could do better than that, and I just spread my bill over a heavy door."

Underground, overground... Buscemi hissed at an errant paper towel. "A secret passage? Seriously? I feel like I skipped the good film and went straight to *Temple of Doom*."

"Call me Short Round if it helps, but figure it out before someone thinks to wonder why two otherwise diffident herons are suddenly going at it in the saloon bar."

Damn, but Drake was a dick. Buscemi didn't need his motivation; she knew Stanley's diversion had bought her a handful of minutes at most. Fine, so she had to be clever, did she?

"Underground passage," she began, swishing her tail in front of her as she sat down. "It needs to be secured against intruders, both deliberate and accidental. If the door really is in here, it needs heavy protection to guard against both accidental discovery and sustained assault. For that you need power. There's no evidence here of significant electrical power, just as well give the room's normal purpose and the human male's documented inability to watch where he's widdling. This is, after all, a *water* closet, and it's long established that electrics and water don't mix.

"So if it can't be electrical... water? Water power?"

Buscemi stopped for a moment, uncertain as to where her reasoning was taking her. "No! That's silly! But logical! You hide an underground passage next to a river by flooding it! Then, to open the passage, you just need to reduce the pressure against the doors!"

She came to a halt in front of Drake, flicking his squashed beak with her tail. "How would you lower water pressure?"

"No clue, blood. I rise above talk of water pressure. Cos I'm a duck. I float, innit?"

Buscemi gave him a curt nod. "There is that. Also, you're indescribably stupid. You can't just flush the toilets? No. There's only two, it would be highly probable that both could be flushed at once by accident and reveal the door inadvertently. The urinals only flush on a timer, and cultists probably aren't the sort to stand around a draughty pub toilet for ten minutes waiting for their next chance to move through. Which just leaves..."

Buscemi and Drake stared up at the six-sided pedestal of washbasins that sprouted mushroom-like from the floor of the impossibly white toilet that was not a toilet. As they stared, a plump drop of water gathered on the spout of one mixer tap. It quivered in the pot pourri-scented air for a brief moment, and Buscemi stared into its depths to see her own face looming large in a distorted reflection of the world.

The drop dripped, elongating slightly as it plummeted from the faucet and fell from sight into the basin. Half a blink later a soft 'spuck' noise drifted down to the duck and the kitten as the water impacted on cold porcelain.

"Why am I staring at a basin?" Drake asked, turning to Buscemi.

But the little detective was already moving.

With a nimble scrabble of her dainty paws against the pedestal, Buscemi hauled herself up level with the taps. "Two toilets. Two urinals. Six sinks. Those two extra sinks are a *safeguard*," she said.

"Safe, man," Drake echoed, completely out of his depth.

With a heavy sigh, Buscemi jumped on to the nearest tap, bringing all her weight to bear on the plunger. As soon as the first drops began to fall, she bounced through the air to land on the neighbouring sink's tap. Under the impact of an excited leaping cat, water gushed into the basin, and Buscemi leapt again.

Purring with delight as she bounced, Buscemi jumped on every tap on the pedestal, until all six were flowing. Then she yowled down to Drake, who was still watching puzzled from the tiled floor. "Come on, it's working!"

Over the roar of water, Drake had trouble hearing this, but he flapped up to the pedestal anyway, standing with

Buscemi on the small flat space that lay between the six basins.

"In what way is it working?" the duck asked after a moment, but quite politely as he couldn't get too far away from Buscemi right now if the feline chose to take offence and decided to deploy her claws.

Buscemi purred as she extended a single claw from one forepaw and reached forward to tap the pedestal with a "plink".

A rumbling gurgle echoed from the pipes in response. The pedestal quivered, and Buscemi swished her tail in triumph. "Going down."

As water filled the basins and flowed into the overflow pipes, the whole pedestal began to sink slowly downwards with a gravelly grinding noise.

"Not cool," squawked Drake, standing up and beating his wings.

"Don't be soft," said Buscemi, "how long did we just spend looking for this? It's far too late to start acting surprised about it now."

The pedestal's column swayed occasionally as they sank ever downward, sending broad loops of slightly soapy water sloshing out over the tiled floor.

About a minute later, they had descended about halfway to the toilet floor. Drake smoothed his ruffled wings back into place. "I now kind of regret freaking back out there. How long's this gonna take?"

Buscemi, who had been enjoying the ride, glanced nervously at the door to the toilets. "That's not an entirely moronic question. We must not be heavy enough to trigger the mechanism properly, they couldn't normally take this long or they'd be interrupted all the time going in and out. So we need to make ourselves heavier, or..."

With a swoosh of water that was barely audible over the gushing basin taps, the urinals all flushed, apparently automatically.

"Yes, that ought to do it," she said. Drake tilted his

head in a puzzled fashion, and then let out a strangled quack as the pedestal gave one lurch, and then plummeted through the floor.

The plunge down the tiled shaft was brief, but when the pedestal finally hit the bottom with a *whoompf*, Buscemi was surprised when she glanced up and saw how far they'd descended. The strip lights of *Ye White Hart*'s gentlemen's toilets must have been a good fifty feet above, shining straight down the hexagonal hole, and helpfully reflected downwards by the smooth white tiles.

A gloomy tunnel stretched away from the pedestal, the top of which had landed, well, flush with the floor. The tiled walls quickly gave way to damp concrete, but as Buscemi and Drake set off along the passage, they realised the framed vintage photographs of ancient Barnes were still hanging from twine hooked over thick rusty nails that had been rammed deep into the walls.

"More tourist tat, even down here," Buscemi yowled as she padded along the uneven floor. Drake half-nodded, then swung his head to look at the photo they'd just passed.

With a concerned quack, he flapped into ungainly flight, and scrabbled with his bill at the print until it fell to the floor with a clatter that echoed all along the dank tunnel.

"Subtle," Buscemi observed with a sardonic twitch of her tail.

Drake motioned her over with one wing. "Save the trash talk, furjob. I don't think anyone's going to be buying *these* as postcards at the OSO."

It was a picture of the traffic island between the Sun Inn, Barnes Pond, and Essex Court Surgery. At first glance the picture was the usual dull thing that humans seemed to like; a photo of somewhere they saw every day, but with less traffic, shorter trees, and fresher paintwork. And yet, where signs advertising the farmer's market now stood, the traffic island was occupied by a large wooden structure, apparently constructed from tightly woven branches. It was surrounded by a dozen or so people who, *weren't* hooded or anything and seemed perfectly normal at first. But then you noticed they *were* mostly wearing large hats, or high collars, and as the figures were pictured mid-cavort around the effigy, it *might* have been coincidence that they were all facing away from the photographer, or had their faces otherwise obscured by waving hands and flapping sleeves.

"The Wicker – what *is* that?" Drake asked, all swagger gone as he stared at the photo with growing unease.

Buscemi sat back on her haunches, not even swishing her tail. "Owl. It's a Wicker... Owl."

"Oh yeah..." that mystery solved, Drake waddled away down the corridor. "This one's the same," he called back, craning his head to examine the next picture along. "But it's later. 1927."

"Is that right?" Buscemi asked idly, her green eyes fixed on the shabby wooden structure, and the dark shape that could just about be seen huddled inside it. She was starting to have some unpleasant instincts about all this, and for once she hoped she was wrong.

"They're all the same! 1934, 1941, 1948, 1955... every, um, *few* years. Then the last one's 1986. Why's that, do you think? Did they get caught? Did they get fed up?"

"Or had they just done enough?"

"What?"

Buscemi shook her head, and trotted down the corridor past Drake, the strange photos strobing past her.

A low roar rumbled all around them. Drake stifled a quack and even Buscemi tensed and flexed her claws nervously. As the noise subsided, a fainter vibration could still be felt in the damp tunnel.

"Must have been the 209 bus," Buscemi whispered, "we've come a long way. I think we must be directly under White Hart Lane."

"I took a perch on one of those things once. It had

spent so long sitting at Mortlake Bus Station that I'd forgotten they were supposed to move. I couldn't hop off like a jittery sparrow when it started moving, not with my rep to maintain. I ended up sitting on the damn thing all the way to Hammersmith, and there's nothing out there but drunk pigeons, piles of burning tyres, and pavement cyclists."

He gradually fell silent under Buscemi's unblinking stare, and the pair continued their softly padding and awkward waddling walks into the darkness.

After a few moments, they reached the end of the tunnel, and faced a heavy fire door. Buscemi turned to Drake. "Right. Now we're not quite sure what we're likely to find beyond this door. So I need you to be ready to sneak in, infiltrate, and steal some camouflaged clothes and stuff. Sound reasonable?"

The duck nodded affably enough. "Duck and cat conspirator uniforms? Why not? So, how do we open *this* door?"

Buscemi rocked back on her hind legs as she looked up at the sturdy door, sitting in a rough brick wall, and very pointedly closed. "You raise an interesting question," she acknowledged.

"We can't just sit and stare at it all night!" Drake snapped, but Buscemi looked thoughtful.

"You'd think not, I must concede, but that's exactly how I get most doors open. In the absence of staff, however... I think this one might be up to you, Drake. Make me proud."

The bird puffed up its plumage for a moment, but then perked up. "OK, I've got this. Whack! Whack! *Whack!*"

After squawking at the top of his lungs, the duck waddled over to one side of the door. Buscemi stared at him in horror. "What the... *dog* was that all about? Have you been eating too much bread or something?"

Drake tilted his head and beckoned her over with one wing, but Buscemi remained crouching on the cold concrete. Then she arched her back as she heard fumbling noises from the other side of the door. "No way," she hissed, and scurried over to join Drake.

As soon as the door creaked open, Drake simply wandered through it. This prompted a murmur of surprise, but no particular alarm, from the brightly lit room beyond. Buscemi took a deep breath, entertained some briefly satisfying thoughts involving crispy duck pancakes, and followed.

"The owls draw living things to feed them, can even spontaneously generate prey. How are these idiots to know we didn't just spawn in the corridor? After all, how likely is it that a sassy streamwise duck and a furjob would just stumble across their secret base?"

Buscemi came as close to boggling as she could without risking her elegant air of mystery. "Sassy? I thought you'd had a head injury."

"Says the cat who wanted to stare at a closed door all night."

Drake seemed pleased with that shot as he swaggered into the thickly carpeted waiting room, lined with that particularly uncomfortable variety of waiting room padded chair. Two jacket and jeans-clad men stood facing them, one with his hand still resting on the door handle.

They didn't seem overly concerned, and Buscemi allowed herself to begin to relax again. That is, until she realised the man holding the door open was none other than Cornetto from Bohemia. Perhaps he wouldn't recognise her?

"Ah, the *clever* kitty at last, I knew she would come through. Fabrice, let our guests through to the inner sanctum."

The bearded Frenchman harrumphed continentally as he stalked the short distance over to the other door, even as Cornetto let go of the door by which they'd entered, which closed smoothly with a decisive *click*.

Buscemi yowled softly. *Botheration.* A riot of thoughts

rampaged through her head, mostly concerning a man who hadn't really seemed to care very much that there had apparently been an execution-style killing in his shop. That was probably a clue to which she ought to have paid a bit more attention. She'd taken his nonchalance to be sheer faith in the justice system not failing an innocent man. Which was a bit odd given that her trials for pooing misdemeanours among the local mouse community tended to end in her summarily eating the defendant before the prosecution had even finished their opening remarks.

Now she realised Cornetto's insouciant shrugs towards the still-warm corpse on his shop floor could be explained just as easily if you thought of him as a man confident that he'd quietly paid some reliable people a lot of money to do some things, then wipe some things, and burn some things, and possibly even break the window, while he made a point of being very visible at an all-night event a solid number of miles away.

"Drake," she purred, "we might need to take out this hipster."

"Blood, do I look like Stanley? What's this clown done to ruffle your feathers, anyway? He called you clever, you lap up that stuff!"

Not for the first time in the last fifteen minutes or so, Buscemi found herself wondering how Stanley was getting on, and wishing it was him down here rather than the enthusiastic but largely useless Drake. She checked herself, this kind of thinking was getting dangerously close to compassion and empathy. Yes, one of her stupid avian acquaintances was marginally more useful than the other, but she had to play the cards she'd been dealt, and there was no need to go around being *uncool* about it, man.

She narrowed her eyes at Cornetto, and swished her tail with menace. To her irritation and mounting unease, he smiled back.

"*Yes*, clever cat, you have run around being so very entertaining. It brought you all the way here to me. And now I know all about your clever friends at the bridge, the library, and rummaging in the local bins."

Buscemi gave her nose a prim lick. "Then I can see, Mr Cornetto, that I have no choice but to kill you all. What a nuisance, I'm not even hungry."

"There it is!" Far from looking like a small terrified rodent, the businessman was leaning towards her, an eager gleam in his eyes. "The judge, the jury, the *executioner*. The arrogance that drove you to set yourself up above the entire animal kingdom. The rage that must burn in your furry little heart. We have been *waiting* for one such as you. You are the vessel that will shape our new world"

He reached out a pudgy forefinger and flicked at her beer bottle badge. The badge that was nothing but a cheap trick to engage her curiosity. A meaningless, worthless piece of litter, that she'd clung to as the validation she'd always… what? Craved? Why? She was Detective Buscemi Daintypaws Twinklefur, what possible need did she have for a human's token of respect?

And what possible need could this human have for her, if not for her deductive prowess and keen sense of justice? Clearly, it wasn't anything she was likely to enjoy. It could even be as bad as the rustling noise of a black bin liner, blowing in the breeze. Her agile mind was full of conflicting emotions, but as Cornetto's finger continued to loom under her nose, both her bright green eyes and all her thoughts converged on it.

She had been manipulated, perhaps. She had certainly been betrayed. She had set her sights on the respect of this sandwich vendor, for some reason. She had a lot of thinking to do. But now, an ill-mannered oaf was waving a finger in her face, and she just wasn't having it.

There was a blur of movement from her very daintiest paw, and Cornetto straightened up with a howl of pain, balling up his apron around his fingers, which were leaking blood.

He stared at her, with murder in his eyes, and she

looked back quite unworried. And very slowly raised her paw to her mouth, and gave her bloodied claws an elegant lick. "Are we done here?"

Cornetto shook a spray of crimson droplets from his hand. "You will go through to the sanctum, *clever* cat. And you will soon come to regret all that your life has been."

Drake quacked derisively. "I don't fink so, bruv."

Fabrice took a step towards them from the open door as though he were thinking of grabbing the intrepid investigators, but he hesitated and blanched when Buscemi hissed at him pointedly.

Her eyes darted around as she weighed up the situation. A trap, then. She should probably have foreseen this eventuality, as she was *such* a darling little cat and superb detective that of course the criminal underworld would seek to enmesh her in all sorts of snares and ambushes.

But the fact remained that, trap or not, through the door lay all the answers for which she'd spent the last few days running around Barnes. Through that door lay the truth. And it was then that Buscemi realised that quite apart from the fame, the ear-tickling, the attention, and the deliciously succulent mice, what she really craved above all else was the truth. She was, after all, a crime-solving cat.

"It's all right, Drake," she said quietly. "It's all right. Without even knowing it, I think I've been staring at this door all my life. I finally decided which side I need to be on."

She looked at him then and saw him properly, the ridiculous posturing mallard who laboured without thanks or payment for his friends all day long. "As ducks go, you're not completely pointless. I don't know what's waiting through that door, but they killed Flollops and 'Ard Ren to get us to this place. You should stay out here."

She turned around before Drake could spoil her tremendously heroic gesture, and padded towards the door.

Cornetto muttered behind her. "Drain her slow, mighty

U-"

"Whack!" Drake said, appearing beside Buscemi with a particularly purposeful waddle. "I can't leave you now, Stanley would go mental. *More* mental."

Together they walked through the door, Buscemi trying to mask her irritation that Drake's noble gesture had stopped her from hearing the name of her adversary. Still, she suspected she'd be hearing it again soon enough.

The two animals paused as they stepped through. No more stuffy underground passages, somehow a huge chamber opened up before them. An uneven concrete floor stretched into the distance, with towering walls of scaffolding lurking on the furthest edges of their vision. The chamber's centre was lit by a single dangling bulb on a long cord from a ceiling that was hidden in shadow even to Buscemi's keen eyes. In that illuminated patch stood a ring of humans, each one carrying, sure enough, an owl sculpted from the world's drabbest plastic.

Buscemi sighed. So here it was. She had to save the humans from their own magpie instincts. The idiots of Barnes had found these things, maybe years ago in some cases, and adorned their homes with them, laughing at the apparent irony of allowing such gaudy ornaments into their carefully tasteful mansions. While all the time the ornaments had been laughing at the true irony of the situation, and quietly drawing the local wildlife to themselves for nourishment. They wore the shape of hunters, but the owls were little more than spiders, each lurking at the centre of a different family and drawing in its prey at its leisure.

"It must be a basement extension," Drake said, almost subdued by the scale of the excavation as they picked their way across the rough surface towards the small crowd, stepping around or over patches of rubble, filthy puddles, discarded tools, and age-hardened wooden beams. "Several floors' worth. We're lucky we got here before they put in the swimming pool and the cinema."

"Yes, well, let's just leave the deductions to the detectives, shall we?" Buscemi had stared at enough scaffolding in her time to recognise a building site, but life in a first floor flat had left her unprepared for the idea that these people might want to bury themselves further in the mud and squalor that their towering buildings suggested they were trying to escape. Staff. It suddenly seemed peculiar to her that she spent so much of her spare time hunting comparatively sane mice and small birds to lay at the thoroughly loopy humans' feet. At least blue tits knew what they wanted from life, even if generally it was just to avoid being eaten by her. But then, for all their stupidity and paradox, humans had somehow invented the tin opener. But then yet again, if they'd had half a brain cell between the entire species, they'd have criminalised catnip decades ago.

"Oh, you sweet summer children. I suppose I'd better save you all." Buscemi looked at the ring of stupefied SW13 residents, each bearing one of the owl effigies. The birds' glassy eyes glinted cruel and hard in the flickering light, a striking contrast to the unfocused vacant stares of the humans. Even Scruffy Staff and Blonde Staff were standing right in front of her, unblinking. Interim Staff was right next to them, bearing her own owl, which had somehow become covered in glitter.

Drake stopped abruptly. Buscemi was about to ask what he was doing, when the duck erupted into flight, clattering up towards the shadowy roof in a loose spiral of chaotic flapping. In a handful of heartbeats, Buscemi was all on her own, facing down a dozen demonic statues and their entranced bearers.

At least I clawed one of 'em, Buscemi thought proudly. *I bet those theatrical luvvie rats couldn't bear to get their paws dirty.*

She reached the middle of the ring, and sat on her haunches, curling her tail around her. "Well," she said. "I'm here."

"Uwila," sang Scruffy Staff. He couldn't carry a note in

a bucket, poor boy.

"If you say so," said Buscemi kindly.

"Uwila," sang Blonde Staff, cutting across Scruffy's tuneless warble to create a discord that made Buscemi's perfect pointy ears swivel.

"Uwila," sang Interim Staff, and Buscemi finally leapt to a conclusion.

"Oh! I know this one! It's that opera song by the butch lad with the vacuum cleaner and the moustache, right? 'Uwila! No! We will not let you go!'"

Her insight was ignored, and indeed contradicted, as the rest of them all started singing "Uwila" over and over again, each apparently picking their own pitch, tempo, and even pronunciation. It was like being mugged by the Welsh language.

All the chanting was beginning to give her a headache, and it was almost a relief when Cornetto stepped forward, and the cacophony subsided to a *sotto voce* mumble. "You see, *clever* cat? For years we have gathered the brightest and purest creatures, and they became one with mighty Uwila, spawning another of her likenesses in effigy. Uwila. The Owl. The epitome of beauty, guile, and ruthless predation. Petrified through the ritual of strigimorphosis, against this glorious day when Uwila might rise again, absorbing the anima of the other silent killer. And now, after the latest offering, the human in my café and the foolish squirrel that was drawn to my paninis just as Uwila demanded sustenance, the hour is finally at hand for her reincarnation!"

"I'm bored, Drake," Buscemi yowled into the rafters. "I tuned out for a bit halfway through all that. I hope you're getting it all?"

Drake quacked loudly from the darkness. "Yeah. I think they're turning you into an owl. Possibly an owl god from the dawn of time. Bit of a result for a ground-glued furjob, I'd have thought."

With a reflexive shudder, Buscemi's bright pink tongue

darted to lick her adorable little black nose. "Turn this masterpiece into a stupid scaly beak? Yeah, right."

"Ahahaha, clever cat," called Cornetto, gloating, and unfazed by the interruption. "Uwila does not need your *permission*, with eleven of her scions gathered. And 'you', as you understand the term, will not be changing into anything. It is only your anima that is required. Your own body, clever cat, will be... well, perhaps after all it is easier just to show you."

Cornetto took a step back into the crowd, which swallowed him in a moment.

"Oh, *flip*," said Buscemi, with feeling. All the owls were glowing with nimbuses of orange light as they were cradled in their owners' arms, and as she spoke, their gimlet eyes all swivelled up and blasted streams of amber fire into the air directly above the particularly intrepid crime-solving cat.

"Gaze at the splendour of Uwila and embrace your destiny," Cornetto called, and his words echoed in Buscemi's head with a tinkle of stardust. The streams of energy converged on a single point just a few feet above the clearing, and as the brilliant feline looked on, an indistinct shape was already taking form at its centre.

The radiance floated downward, and the shape at its glowing epicentre began to move, unfurling sleek wings from its body, glistening talons lowering from the shimmering haze. So this thing was going to eat her soul or something? She could really use some commentary here so she could work out how to get out of this.

Cornetto obliged. "Uwila comes! Freed from her timeless prison in the darkness of Miron at last, to feast on the essence of the last pure soul in the Barnes peninsula!"

Buscemi licked her forepaws and gave her ears a dab, as close to nervous as she was ever likely to admit. Pure soul, though. Seemed a shade unlikely but she'd take it as a compliment. Stick that in your floppy ear, Puddles.

"Feed on the sacrifice, great Uwila!" Cornetto

bellowed.

"Ready to bring the pain," called Drake.

"Aaagggcchhhh!" screamed the shape, arching its feathery back at the heart of the unearthly glow. It flexed its talons, and fixed Buscemi with a predatory glare from its piercing eyes. Its enormous black pupils were a bottomless abyss of primal terror.

Buscemi swished her tail, and stared right back into the abyss. "Did someone just say this cocky sparrow bust out of prison?"

"In the darkness of Miron," Drake called down happily, then dodged sharply as Cornetto pitched a half-brick at him. "Whack!"

Buscemi met the owl's baleful glower head-on with her most mocking stare. "Well, how about that? Couldn't do your stir, little birdie? Time you were sentenced to solitary confinement... in my belly!"

Uwila lunged downwards faster than thought. She hit the ground in a bundle of glowing plumage, wings swooping and claws fastening on a furry shape that was abruptly elsewhere.

Buscemi was sitting on the other side of the ring, idly inspecting her forepaw. "Oh dear. You're one *slow* feather-brain."

"That's racist!" Drake yelled as he circled the rafters in unsteady flight, trying to find a safe roosting spot.

"Busy," Buscemi called back as the owl's form shimmered and in a blink the tangled ball of feathers was facing her, wings spread wide. The owl was unscathed apart from a murderous glint that had appeared in its enormous eyes. Its head bobbed as its ears fixed her position in the dim light.

Owls. Weaknesses. Buscemi's mind raced. The streets of Barnes were pretty bio-diverse, but somewhat lacking on the owl front. No sense of smell, she dimly remembered, but she was pretty sure rubbing herself against Cornetto's grubby chinos wouldn't fool a supernatural entity from the dawn of prehistory in any case.

Uwila lunged forward again, talons raking, but she was slow from a standing start, and Buscemi simply bounced into the air.

"Twit twoo, swivelhead," she purred as she sailed over the glowing owl, and raked her claws daintily down the plumage on its back. It snarled, but not through any obvious injury.

Buscemi landed on all four paws, naturally, and charged straight at Uwila. As she'd ~~anticipated, the bird~~ leapt ~~straight back into~~ the air to try and take her. As it soared upward, Buscemi corkscrewed on her own dive and reached up with one adorable razor sharp claw to cut off a single feather with an inaudible, but still tangible *snick*.

The single downy feather fluttered from the bird's undercarriage, to a gasp from the assembled brainwashed residents of Barnes. It floated to a landing between Buscemi's gently twitching ears, where it seemed to lodge like a baleful third eye.

"Yes, that's first blood to me," said Buscemi gently, "and next time you lads want to raise a primordial chaos deity, just take a moment to think, 'but is it *right for Barnes*'?"

Uwila shimmered again, and flowed from a tangled mess of wings to a sage old bird with a primly-pursed hooked beak. She tilted her head very slightly, and with a streak of light, she was in the rafters next to Drake.

"Oh *man*, I *knew* this was getting out of hand," the duck quacked in a plaintive tone. "Can you get up here?"

Buscemi wagged her tail in irritation. "What do *you* think? You might be a shifty reed-bummer, but I have to admit you've kind of got the edge on me with all this flying stuff." She paused, aware of the crowd's gaze fixating on her endearingly decorated head. "At least you did... until I had... the Magic Feather!"

As Uwila drifted menacingly towards Drake, Buscemi

screwed her eyes tightly shut, and gave her nose a quick lick in concentration.

"Yes!" shouted Cornetto from somewhere at the back of the crowd of onlookers. "Use the power! Draw ever closer in union with Dread Uwila!"

"Whack! Do something!" The glowing owl was barely a foot away from the panicked duck as he shuffled along a thin wooden beam. Its hooked beak winched open.

"I'm a giant feathery bumhole with maggoty talons," it said in a matter-of-fact voice. Drake cocked his head at it.

"Say *what*, blood?"

Uwila's eyes had widened even further, if that was possible, as though astonished at its own utterances. It opened its beak again, and began to screech...

...and then Buscemi stood in its place, looking very pleased with herself, a glowing feather blazing from its position tucked safely behind her ear.

The cat looked down, realised she was standing in mid-air, and thrashed all four paws until she was standing on the beam next to Drake. Which probably shouldn't have worked. She swished her tail in triumph.

Drake sighed. "All right. Be clever. How did you do that?"

With a contented purr, Buscemi indicated the scene below with her forepaw. "If they really did pick me out for all this, I guessed Uwila was already attuned to me, that was the whole point of putting that creepy statue in the flat, after all. I just had to turn the tables by getting a piece of the owl, and then tuning my own brainwaves into it."

Down below, the crowd stirred as Uwila lay sprawled in the centre of the ring, flailing a single wing in vague circles and looking a bit concussed.

"As easy as that?" Drake asked. "Looked to me like you just got lucky. A feather just landed on your head and you squinted like you were trying to hold in a fart."

Buscemi sniffed. "I keep telling you. I happen to be an extremely clever and resourceful cat."

They both looked down again. Drake bobbed his head. "I hope you are, bruv, cos that owl's getting up, and her clown look *pissed.*"

Sure enough, Uwila was back on her feet and looking a lot less drunk, casting about for her prey at ground level. And Cornetto was staring straight up at them with eyes full of naked bloodlust.

"Mighty Uwila, end this game. Your tribute is cornered. The clever kitty awaits on high!"

The owl's head swivelled up sharply to scan the rafters as Buscemi turned to Drake. "He's a jumped-up waiter who thinks he's an entrepreneur, of *course* he looks cross. Now, I can't use the bird's own powers too much or it absorbs me by proxy and a new dark age spreads over the Barnes peninsula as far south as Roehampton. Where they won't even notice the difference. But the bird is, for all the magic and murder, basically just a bird. By which I mean it's thicker than puppy poo."

"That's racist," Drake snapped for the second time that evening.

Uwila flapped its wings and launched itself into an upward glide that was far swifter than it had any aerodynamic right to be.

Buscemi twitched an ear as the glowing golden owl darted up towards them. Then she bared her teeth. "Scruffy Staff plays a whole lot of video games," she said, by way of non-explanation.

Drake frowned. "Wha? WHACK!" Buscemi reared up and swatted the mallard from his perch with a mighty double-pawed swipe.

The tumbling swearing duck collided with the blazing soaring owl in a flash of light. Drake was blown clean across the chamber, his plumage smouldering. Meanwhile Uwila hurtled straight towards the ceiling, her feathers blazing brighter than ever as she shrieked in rage.

Buscemi carried on talking as though Drake was still beside her, rather than flying sideways through the chamber at breakneck speed towards a solid wall. "You see, in theory she could reorient herself towards me in a twinkling, mid-flight, and not lose a shred of momentum. I'd be dead. But she's *slow* with prey that can fight back, she can barely rationalise in three dimensions after an eternity trapped inside crappy statues, and thanks to me flattening her delta waves like a *boss* through the neural link provided by this feather – uh oh -"

Uwila soared into a crossbeam high above even the rafters where Buscemi was perched. There was a *clunk* and another explosion of golden light.

Instead of rebounding, Uwila dropped like a stone towards the floor, and the circle of Barnes residents. Beak first.

"Hey, Cornetto!" Buscemi yelled down to *Bohemia*'s proprietor. "The cake is a lie, *clever waiter*!"

The man's face was a mask of terror as Uwila plummeted towards him, her beak stretched wide open greedily. "Clever kitty!" he cried.

Uwila struck, and a violent shockwave shook the whole chamber as a shower of golden sparks erupted from the blazing owl and her accidental victim.

Brick dust and concrete fragments cascaded from the ceiling, and Buscemi clung to her thin wooden perch with every ounce of strength in her delicate velvety paws.

As the sparks and smoke cleared, Uwila was again left reeling on the floor, to another rumble of discontent from the owl statue larceny-prone citizens of Barnes. There was no sign of their ringleader, except a very small puddle of grease where the owl now stood.

Buscemi wrinkled her adorable nose. Now things were tricky. Taking out Cornetto had removed the conscious villain of the piece, but there was the small matter of a narked owl god from the dawn of history who'd just absorbed a human soul, and would no doubt be drunk on the power rush just as soon as she got her bearings. It was all up to Detective Daintypaws now. She had to get down there, and finish this. But how? While she was always more than confident of landing on her four velvety paws, that wouldn't do her much good if she fell from such a great height that said paws were smashed straight through her bum on impact.

"Whaaaack! What the *goose* you playing at, bruv? I just flattened my beak on that damn wall!" Drake had flown back to their beam, and was beating his wings in a game attempt at hovering as he bobbed and lurched in front of her.

Buscemi flashed her teeth in the closest she could currently be bothered to get to a smile. "Hello, ducky! Perfect timing."

She jumped for Drake's neck, claws outstretched, and chuckled at the bird's desperate attempt to dodge. She sailed through the short stretch of empty air and grabbed at his absurd spindly-yellow legs, just as a streaming blast of sparkling golden magical energy obliterated the chunk of timber on which she'd just been standing.

"Going down," she purred.

Down turned out not to be a problem. Drake thrashed his wings wildly to try and keep them airborne, shaking his feet as hard as he dared to try and dislodge Buscemi. Her claws tensed instinctively from gripping his legs to really digging in, and he settled for doing his best to slow their descent.

When they were still ten feet from the stone floor, Buscemi decided to do the fowl a favour and jumped down. As she fell, a second blast of energy sliced through the air where she'd been clinging just moments previously. Uwila was growing impatient. And a good deal more accurate.

It goes without saying that Buscemi landed on all four of her soft velvet paws, her tail thumping down behind her and throwing up a large puff of dust from the rough concrete. Superhero landing, oh *yes*.

She raised her head, and her newly golden eyes blazed

with primal magic. Cornetto's lifeforce flooded through Uwila, and into her via the feather conduit. The shifty hipster had given them both equal power. She could end this. As long as she didn't lose her own soul in the process.

Uwila beat her wings, answering the challenge in the intrepid cat's golden stare.

"I... am a god," Buscemi said in a tone of wonder.

Circling above, Drake scoffed. "Someone read your Christmas list." He quailed as Buscemi growled back at him, a roar of primal fury with only the faintest trace of her plaintive croaky miaow resonating at the edges.

"Keep it together, furjob," he warned, dipping low. "Your man back there *wanted* you to use its power, you'll burn!"

What was the point of having the power of a god if you couldn't use it? Buscemi could feel it fizzing through her body, all that potential energy. She could obliterate Uwila, turn her into a second smoking grease stain on the chamber floor with a twitch of her tail. But then she'd simply replace the owl, she realised. She looked down at her dainty paws, and almost panicked as she saw the tiniest downy feathers beginning to sprout between her claws. That's why Uwila hadn't pressed the attack. All she had to do was wait.

Buscemi shook her head in frustration. She was an extremely pretty and clever little cat, too cunning by far to be beaten by hipster scum and his magic budgie. There had to be another way.

As she shook her head, her bottle cap detective badge, already dislodged by Cornetto's clumsy fingers, fell from her collar, and spun on its edge on the ground with a gentle tinkling noise.

Uwila's eyes narrowed on the battered chunk of metal, and even some of the transfixed Barnes residents seemed to search blindly in the direction of the noise.

Buscemi watched the wave of consternation sweep the room, confused. The badge's spin slowed, and the bottle top finally fell on to its side. A bold red star looked up at her. And Buscemi realised Uwila wasn't the only higher power in the room.

"People of Barnes," she growled, her voice echoing around the vast space with an odd resonance. "Disperse and be about your business. There is nothing to see here. I repeat, there is nothing to see here."

The former bearers of Uwila's effigies shuddered, and blinked, and were awake again. They looked around in confusion and alarm, and began to mutter among themselves.

"That's right," called Buscemi. "Make your way to the exit, please, there is nothing to see here. This area is not safe."

They looked around, Scruffy and Blonde staff looking the most confused among them as they no doubt wondered why their small black cat had suddenly started bellowing at them in a dim underground bunker.

"They don't understand," Buscemi whispered, her whiskers drooping as Uwila hooted in triumph and leapt into the air, circling the small crowd as though picking her first victim.

Then Drake soared from the rafters, quacking his little heart out.

"This way, you over-mortgaged berks," he squawked, flying low over their heads, and diving down towards the door that led to the underground tunnel. "Whack, whack, whack!"

"Look, a duck!" Blonde Staff shouted, and the crowd followed Drake, still half-dazed.

Uwila screeched in rage as they shuffled towards the door, diving with her golden claws outstretched at the elderly children's book writer who was bringing up the rear.

Buscemi winced, but free of their trance it seemed the owl had no power over the humans. Its claws passed harmlessly through the author's back and Uwila crashed to the ground in a ball of feathers, the people of Barnes stepping over and through her without even noticing.

"Uwila," she purred, and the owl stopped trying to right itself and merely swivelled her head until her huge, mad, ancient eyes were staring straight into Buscemi's own.

"I am arresting you on suspicion of the murders of Flollops the Squirrel and 'Ard Ren the fox, for incitement to civil unrest in the Barnes area, and for absconding from the darkness of Miron. You do not have to say anything -"

"Eckkkkk!" screamed Uwila, but she seemed stuck to the floor.

"-but anything you do say will be written down and may be used in evidence against you," Buscemi finished, wishing she had a pen. "Or, ah, I might have to just remember it."

The star on her badge shone brilliant red. She could never remember the bit about lawyers.

"Skip to the end… I arrest you *in the name of the LAW*!"

Uwila flapped her wings in sudden panic as a bright red column of light erupted from the badge. The column shot towards the ceiling, forcing Drake to swerve in the air to avoid it, before bending, looping, coiling… and striking.

The bird finally made an attempt to leap into the air, but a thick coil of red energy snagged her firmly by one leg. Buscemi stared on proudly as Uwila was dragged, thrashing and screeching back towards her badge.

As the owl neared the circle of light around Buscemi's badge, she seemed to grow smaller and smaller, her hoots and screeches more desperate and shrill, and her wings on the point of snapping.

Finally, her tiny foot touched the star, and with a final hiss of defiance at Buscemi, she vanished.

Drake touched down for a surprisingly controlled landing next to the brave cat. "You're nicked, bruv," he quacked, as a thin tendril of smoke curled up from the badge. "What now, furjob?"

"I don't know," said Buscemi, "I just want to know if it's safe to pick up my badge."

With a squawk of triumph, Stanley soared through the doorway, before tumbling to their feet in a tangle of limbs that was still somehow full of grace and poise. He was panting, and his plumed crest was even more awry than usual.

Drake tried not to look too concerned. "All sorted, bruv?"

With the most disdainful squawk, Stanley surged to his feet with only the faintest wobble to show for his recent exertion, towering over Drake and Buscemi. "Sorted? Was the outcome in doubt, tha' shifty soft buggers?"

"Not at all," Buscemi said, with the slightest inclination of her head, "but we've not exactly been idle down here while we waited for you to plant a webbed foot in Derek's cloaca."

With a worried glance at the golden feather that was still tucked behind Buscemi's ear, Stanley deflated. "I know. Between Derek's - ah, confession - and the sudden stream of hoity-toity southerners heading to the gents' lavs, I got the gist. Where's Uwila? I'm under standing orders from the Council as to how many pieces to tear that bleeder in the event of her manifestation within my borough."

His eyes narrowed, his crest bobbing up and down as they did so. "No, really. Where's the vengeful primordial owl god, and why has it let a Deathless Guardian yammer on so long?"

The heron's regal beak drooped to follow Buscemi and Drake's guilty gaze right down to the bottle top on the concrete floor, which pulsed gently with golden light.

"You didn't." Stanley's voice was hoarse with shock, and an edge that Buscemi found hard to read. Was it awe? Or menace? Or even fear?

Either way she felt distinctly defensive for some reason. "In your absence, I was forced to improvise. Ms Uwila has been detained, pending further charges. I suppose your Council could extradite her, but I would like my badge back at some point."

Stanley looked up, and his eyes were if anything wilder than when he'd faced Derek. "Your badge? Eh, unlikely. Little cat, you *arrested* a higher being that's been imprisoned throughout the length of human history. Have you any idea how absurd that is?"

Buscemi bit back a joke about the absurdity of humans having such a sophisticated thing as history, she felt rather that her crime-solving professionalism was being called into question. "I did it properly," she pointed out, in an acid tone. "Read the mad birdie her rights, I didn't even try and eat her feet or anything."

"An irresistible force meets an immovable object," Stanley mused, without clarifying which was which. "Interesting. Where the blinking heck are we, anyway?"

"Under some house," Drake supplied. "I definitely heard that waiter guy banging on about us being 'beneath the citadel of the Welsh bard', whatever that means."

Buscemi brightened. "Oh! It's probably Duffy! Duffy lives round here. I like Duffy, her music's... compelling."

Stanley's expression was grim. "Whoever's house we're under. I hope their insurance is good."

As he spoke, the badge rose from the floor in a cloud of golden light, shaking and spitting fat crimson sparks.

Buscemi licked her nose. "Ah. Should we... vacate the area?"

"Nay mither yerself, little cat. The lift's full of ponces and we're stuck at ground zero of a cataclysm of primal magic. We're jiggered, my brave buggers. But we did save the Barnes peninsula and possibly even Roehampton from a thousand years of feudal blood magic rule."

Drake's voice was hollow. "Yeah, bruv. Wicked."

The badge glowed brighter. Smoke began to curl from its crinkly lower edges. Buscemi crouched down and stared at the levitating bottle top. Until the last few moments it had been her proudest achievement, and even though it was now dooming her, it still made her want to purr.

Uwila's power still fizzed through her veins, and an angry hooting was building in her mind. If she used that power, she could save Drake and Stanley from the imminent conflagration. But, she realised with a shiver, that was exactly what Uwila's last sane remnant was hoping for. She would be lost, her soul swept aside by the tsunami of primal energy that would course through her. Uwila would be free. Buscemi would have failed. Drake and Stanley would live. Flollops and 'Ard Ren would be avenged. She would never eat tuna again. Wow. No wonder cats had little truck with ethics, this was some intense stuff.

A stream of golden fire blasted from the badge up into the rafters, and Buscemi raised a hesitant paw. "I… I think I might be able to do you a favour."

Both birds performed a double take at her.

"It's no bother," said Stanley kindly, before taking a graceful step to the left as a small shower of plaster dust trickled down to where he had been standing.

A half-brick crashed into the same spot a moment later.

"It's draughty on that river, all the fish taste slightly of diesel, and a hard winter's coming on. We'll stop here, if it's all the same to you."

Drake lowered his beak. "He's trying to say, we stand together on this, furjob."

The ground began to shake, and more rubble crashed to the ground. Buscemi's wide green eyes began to stream from the building heat from the badge. This was it, the end of everything. But she had cracked a proper case, right in front of everyone! She was, in the end, a true crime-solving cat.

"What a touching scene," drawled a smooth voice behind the three of them. "It almost seems a pity that I must now save you all."

As Buscemi, Drake and Stanley turned to stare in

surprise into the blazing eyes of Dave the Impaler, Buscemi reeled from a stone that struck her little head.

"Little cat!" shouted Stanley, and his voice seemed to echo in her head even louder than Uwila's mad hoot.

"Time for a cat nap," she tried to say brightly, but her voice seemed to slur thickly as even the blazing golden fire looked dim and hazy. The stones tumbling from the roof looked more like boulders now, but she couldn't seem to remember why that was all a bad thing.

Her dainty but reliable paws failed, her legs collapsed into jelly beneath her, and she folded to the floor. Some people seemed to be making a fuss somewhere, but that was someone else's problem. She needed to snooze.

She purred gently as cold hands picked her up and wrapped her in some cloth. She blinked, slowly, and when her eyes opened she was interested to see that she was now being carried upwards through the air, bobbing here and there to avoid falling debris. As her eyelids drooped closed for another really long blink, she even noticed that there was a golden fireball chasing at her paws as they rose through the air.

This is probably quite exciting, she thought, as she closed her eyes.

8 BLACK CATS AND REVELATIONS

Buscemi woke to feel cold slates under her fur. She wrinkled her adorable nose as she took in the stink of brackish brick dust and soot that covered her. She licked her forepaw and was about to give her ears a good wash when she heard low voices nearby.

Cautiously, she cracked open one eye, pleased to discover that it was still dark, at least. She was on a rooftop somewhere near the river, she could hear the gloop and slosh of the dark waters somewhere below. There was also the faintest whiff of burnt charcoal and stale beer. *The White Hart?* Still?

"How can you be a deathless guardian of Barnes Bridge *and* Hammersmith Bridge?" Drake was asking Stanley as the two birds perched side by side on the precarious chimney overlooking Lower Richmond Road. They both contemplating a smoking crater on the other side of the road, where Buscemi was fairly sure a large house had stood just a few hours previously. "There's over a mile between them! Even as the duck flies."

The heron shrugged, always an expansive gesture with such a long neck. "Them's the rules, lad. I should have thought about it before I leathered Derek. But now I've won, I'm stuck wi' Barnes. I could hand on Hammersmith, though, to the right bird."

"That's jokes, man! There's no other heron comes near Hammersmith Bridge! They're all terrified of you!"

There was a certain air of satisfaction in the way Stanley tossed his plumed head. "Aye? That's as maybe, the soft buggers, but I do know another *bird* as drops by, come what may, rain or shine…"

There was a long pause while Stanley let that sink in. Drake quacked about in confusion, and Buscemi was ready to scream by the time the penny finally dropped.

"What?" he squawked. "I'm no heron. *And* I'm a bloody idiot, you said so yourself."

"Aye lad, you're a hopeless wazzock. But that's never been a bar to high office in this land. And the Guardian Council can lump it – they've let blinking *cormorants* take on Blackfriars and Tower Bridge anyway – I need someone I can trust. That Uwila bleeder didn't seem the type to take no for an answer. If they could get to Derek… I need a dimwit I can trust *and* oversee, if you get my drift? Not to mention we've a blinking vampire on the prowl, and we owe it a favour after it hoicked us all out of there. I don't want the Guardians sticking their oar in round here until we've got that bad bit of business straightened out. No, I need someone I can keep an eye on, young duck."

Buscemi thought that sounded a raw deal; all that responsibility, but obviously still just taking orders from Stanley. What did she care, though? She was tired, and she wanted a cushion to knead. She mewed softly at the thought of sleeping for a week.

The two birds were at her side in a moment.

She yawned, delicately, and rolled to her dainty paws, pushing out her front legs and giving her spine a really good stretch as she braced her paws against the firm roof slates.

"He wouldn't leave you," said Drake. "Even after the vampire flew off. He said that's the whole point of being a

Deathless Guardian. Being the comfort strangers can rely on."

"After all this, you're hardly strangers," she protested. "When I think of what we've been through together these last few days. Your bravery, your loyalty: busting me out of house arrest, challenging Derek, snooping around for clues for all those hours on end? No, you're no strangers…"

Drake's chest was puffed up fit to burst, and even Stanley had a certain jaunty swagger as he lifted one leg from the ground and tucked it behind his other knee.

Buscemi continued. "I'm hardly prone to saying things like this, but I think it really needs to be said. You two have become, to me, well, almost like…"

"Friends?" said Drake.

"Family?" said Stanley.

Buscemi let their suggestions hang in the air for a moment, before cocking her head at a slightly quizzical angle.

"Hardly. You've become almost like… yes. Staff."

"Staff?" the two birds chorused together in disbelief.

"You're welcome," the little black cat said lightly, and began washing her ears.

She ignored the frosty silence from Drake and Stanley, and after a moment, already bored, she hopped down from the roof to a convenient windowsill.

As she looked down at the street, she heard a whispered commotion above her.

"… that's her attitude, well, I'm not carrying her back upriver," said Drake.

"Oh, no need," said Buscemi sweetly. "I'll get the bus home."

"The bus?" Stanley repeated in a hollow tone.

"Yes, I'll hop on the 209 from Barnes Bridge. I gather it's very quick, especially this early in the morning."

"They'll let you on without a ticket?"

Buscemi frowned, for a Deathless Guardian, Stanley really was a very obtuse bird. "Why of course not, that would be very silly, unprofessional, and remiss of them. No, I shall grace them with the opportunity to bear me home."

She saw a bus approaching down Mortlake High Street. "Now, if you could just lend a wing to get me down to the first floor, I think I can jump to the picnic tables from there. In your own time, but also kind of nowish."

***

Out on the draughty balcony, the staff stepped nervously away from the food bowl after emptying the entire tin of tuna into it. Buscemi stared at them both for a long moment, before the smell of briny fish became too much and she lowered her head to tuck in. She heard Blonde Staff take a deep breath, as though about to speak, but then she sighed and the two of them stepped back inside the flat.

They had said nothing about how they had come to find themselves on the site of Duffy's basement extension, or about what had happened to their latest bit of ornamental tat. They had spent that first morning in a bit of a daze, truth be told, and they were so out of it that they were even voluntarily watching *The Big Bang Theory*, even though Buscemi knew for a fact there was perfectly good *Columbo* on another channel.

Puddles was growing ever bolder, so the staff had started leaving her food on the far side of the balcony fence, so he couldn't get at it. It was a humiliation, of course, but it meant Buscemi could eat with all the peace and concentration that the noble art of lunchtime demanded. It was a sensible compromise.

Buscemi didn't much care for compromises, ordinarily. But she did like tuna, and after licking the bowl clean, she wandered inside the flat in a relatively good-natured mood.

The puppy was lying on the living room rug, gnawing on an old bone the staff had given him, with quiet determination. Buscemi considered hissing and swiping at his nose, but her good mood had set her thinking. He *had* distracted the staff from getting that bell, after all, and helped her bust out of the flat. He was unspeakably vulgar and graceless, of course, but perhaps not irredeemably horrific.

"You know, Puddles," she said. "You were pretty solid back there. If I was a drooling moron like you, I might even feel like I owed you one."

The bone dropped from the tiny dog's jaws, as he fixed his soulful brown eyes on Buscemi. "Oh, in-chew-bitably," he said.

THE END

Buscemi will return in
Detective Daintypaws: Murder in the China Express!

Bonus Recipe: *Thon à la Boîte*

Preparation time: 5 minutes
Cooking time: 0 minutes
Serves: 1 hungry cat

1. Take a tin of tuna and open it, however you humans manage that sorcerous act. Drain off the oil or brine, and tip the tuna into a small bowl.
2. Flake the tuna with a fork, and season well with any bits of chicken fat or chorizo you might happen to have lying around.
3. Woah, cowboy. *Plenty* of chorizo, all right? What, did we lose a *war*? That's better. Good lad.
4. Garnish with a sprig of coarse paté, if liked. I like.
5. Serve immediately, with a fresh bowl of water.
6. Take at least ten steps away from both bowls and look out of the window for four minutes. What? No one's going to eat with you staring at them, making cute noises and acting like I ought to be grateful or something.

Repeat steps 1-6 nightly.

ABOUT THE AUTHOR

A lifelong Doctor Who and science-fiction fan, Andrew Lawston writes in a variety of genres and media, from science-fiction plays to translations of 18th Century French literature. He is also a recovering teacher, a playwright, and an experienced actor. His King Lear was the toast of Croydon, wherever that is.

A Barnes resident for ten years, Andrew now lives in West London with his wife and, of course, their crime-solving black cat, Buscemi. Now fifteen years old and still going strong, Buscemi has given this work her tentative endorsement by glowering intently at the laptop screen at various stages of the book's composition.

BY THE SAME AUTHOR

Something Nice – 10 Stories (2012)
Something Nicer (2015)
Apocalypse Barnes (2017)
Zip! Zap! Boing! (2018)
The Frag Prince (2018)
Voyage Of The Space Bastard (2018)
Rudy On Rails (2018)

Printed in Great Britain
by Amazon